MERMAID VOICES

Poetry and prose from
Medway Mermaids
Women's Writing Group 2022

Michele Bottomer

Published in 2022 by FeedARead.com Publishing

First Edition

A CIP catalogue record for this title is available from the British Library.

MERMAID VOICES

Poetry and prose from
Medway Mermaids
Women's Writing Group 2022

It is with great pleasure that we publish our latest anthology of work. This book is presented in four parts with work by members and friends of our group. We chose WATER for our main theme, with our mermaid voices expressing thoughts, relating tales, and speaking of many places, real and imagined. Writing developed from short word-count exercises into longer stories and members' own poetry.

In our writing group, everyone's voice is relevant and heard. Mermaids listen to each other without judgement. We don't set standards, but allow all to grow and learn at their own pace. The result is this book, our second such collection, containing a delightful mix of creative writings which we hope you will enjoy.

This book is dedicated to the memory of LIZ TREDGET

Any profits from the sales of this book will be donated to the
Motor Neuron Disease Association, who work to make a world free from
MND. Every little helps.
If you would like to contribute further, or if you have borrowed the book
or bought it second-hand, the MNDA would really appreciate it. They are
fantastic in their support of sufferers and their carers:
http://www.justgiving.com/remember/951178/Liz%20-Tredget

The editing team on this book were:
Susan Pope, Judith Northwood-Boorman, and Brenda M Moss.

Cover art by: Catriona Murfitt
Interior graphics by: Judith Northwood-Boorman/Canva.com

Foreword

by Fiona Sinclair.

This is an anthology that surprises and delights the reader. It is at times playful and at other times deeply moving. What strikes the reader is the writers' affinity with the water, and their skill at broadening their focus to examine it in all its mediums from tears to a tsunami.

The collection is divided into four sections. The first deals with the notion of the mermaid as motif, the second moves onto darker contemporary concerns, the third then offers relief, with playful pieces and the final section offers works that are personal to each writer. Every section includes poetry and prose and the theme of water flows throughout the sections.

In the first part we are introduced to the idea of mermaids who are described in exquisite language 'Her hair dazzled like a thousand sunsets'; these are fantastical creatures as at home in their element as dolphins. Yet as fabulous as they are in themselves, beneath the surface of these poems and short stories lie some serious truths. A seemingly disabled grannie is in fact a mermaid who craves the liberation of swimming thereby hinting at the restrictions the disabled face in life. A fisherman voyeuristically observes a mermaid, the shocking final lines hinting darkly at male control and coercion. The section then broadens out to examine water itself as an element. It becomes a metaphor for anger. The Sea Horse becomes a meditation on evolution. Many of the prose pieces are satisfying flash fiction that pack a punch. Often the simplest poems bear deeper truths, for example, something as simple as a child learning to skim stones on water becomes a life lesson that our actions have consequences.

Part two becomes darker, broadening out the theme to examine geo-political and ecological concerns. Water becomes a destructive force in pieces vividly describing the human cost of tsunamis. Narratives are deployed to examine our negative impact on the earth. Folklore and myth are used again to hold up a mirror to the toxicity of modern life. The plight of migrants is handled sensitively. Here vignettes are a powerful way of giving a snapshot of the horrors endured by many. The sea becomes both a barrier and a boundary to those escaping war and famine. Excellent writer's craft is used to navigate such big issues. A woman's 'sea green eyes' are used to evoke the memory of a migrant's horrifying journey to the UK.

Section three then judiciously lightens the tone and subject matter. Many poems concentrate on wildlife associated with water from dragonflies to baby turtles which make the reader smile. Water in all its forms is celebrated, including the course of a waterfall. A sense of place is often summoned throughout the anthology, generally associated with the sea or rivers. Margate becomes somewhere that reminds the elderly character of the first meeting with a loved one, now dead. This prose piece sensitively reminds us that such meaningful places can bring comfort.

The final section builds on the idea of what it means to be female, more specifically a woman of a certain age in the 21st century. Tribute is paid to a dear friend now struck down with MND but whose collection of shoes evokes her glorious personality. There is a constant call for older women to reject the societal expectation of becoming grey and invisible. Life, we are reminded is for the living and should be embraced with gusto. The subject of one poem prefers to be purple rather than beige. Reportage is well used to share with the reader such life-affirming events as a trip on the Orient Express. Yet the downside of ageing is also acknowledged in some tender pieces examining the effects of dementia on both the patient and the partner. Memoir is effectively used in this section, reinforcing perhaps the importance of our memories, and reminding us of a lost world of antimacassars.

The final poem is very well placed and seems to sum up the collection. It advises the reader to:

> Express and enrich yourself as well as others,
> Look within to grasp the opportunities,
> Share and start joyful living.

This is an apt message for the times we live in and is certainly a modus operandi that these writers live by. This is evident in the original and insightful works that make up this entertaining and thought-provoking anthology. What strikes the reader too, is that these 'Mermaids 'have certainly learnt their craft.

About Fiona Sinclair.
Fiona is a poet who lives near Faversham. She was a teacher for over 25 years and returned to writing on retirement. Fiona has 10 pamphlets and collections published. She enjoys reading for the Mermaid writing group

from her new works. They in turn enjoy her witty and insightful poems about love, life, and the joys of being a middle-aged 'rock chick'.

Fiona Sinclair's publications include:

Ladies who lunch. Lapwing Press 2014
Slow Burner. Smokestack Press 2018
The Time Traveller's Picnic. Dempsey and Windle Press. 2019
Greedy Cow. Smokestack Press 2021
Second Wind. Dempsey and Windle Press 2022.

A few words from our contributors.

Susan Pope
It has been a privilege to lead Medway Mermaids' Women's Writing Group for over 15 years. Members continue to come and go, but our writing ethic remains the same: if you love creative writing – you're one of us, no matter if you are a published author or just beginning your writing journey. We welcome all as part of our writing community, offering support and inspiration to women who want to write. Like the mermaids of folklore, modern independent women have much to say about their lives and the world around them. We strive to inspire members to speak out with their individual voices and tell their stories.

Susan's publishing history: Lighter Than Air 2008, Murder at Chatham Grande (as editor) 2013, Bedtime Stories for Grown-Ups 2013, Spirit of the Jaguar 2017, Short Story, The Boy on the Beach, Refugees and Peacekeepers, 2017. The Power of Wings 2020.

Ann Smith
When I attended secondary school many years ago, I wrote a short story that had the teacher praising my effort. She entered it into a writing competition, and even though I wasn't shortlisted, the idea of writing was firmly planted. It was over six decades later that I found the Medway Mermaids and with their encouragement started to put that childhood dream into practice. Now with two Lucy novellas, children's stories, poetry collections and jottings later, I am so grateful to the Mermaids writing group for their continued support. Thank you.

Publishing history: Criminal Love 2018. The Trouble with being Married, Making Waves, 2020. A Strange Kind of Madness 2021. Rhymes that make you say Ooh Hah and Yuk 2022

Nilufar Imam
I was born in a professional family interested in literature during the British Raj. A fortunate childhood trip to London in 1950 for two years and attending a school in Chiswick sparked my love of poetry. Returning to East Pakistan I completed my medical qualifications and travelled to England in March 1963 for pursuing the professional path until retirement in 2000. A miraculous encounter with the chairman of The Medway Mermaids in 2017 opened a new direction. I joined as a member of the group. Their encouragement provided confidence culminating in my self-publishing four books of which three consist of poetry.

Publishing history: Feelings Revealed. 2018, Ma -A Trailblaze. 2018, Despair, Dream Delight. 2018, Bangladesh Home of the Royal Bengal Tiger 2021, Searching for the Rainbow. 2022.

Pauline Odle

I have enjoyed creative writing since 2012. I particularly like writing poetry, historical fiction, and memoir, as my favourite interest is social history. Mermaids give me the chance to explore different genres, and meet other creative writers, and authors. Mermaids certainly kept my creative brain working during the lockdowns.

Michele Barton Macintosh

In 2014, I had the privilege of meeting Susan Pope and joining Medway Mermaids. Since I was a small child, I have dreamt of being a writer, yet I never had the opportunity, or the courage, until I joined this group. I would like to thank you for choosing to read our book. I hope it brings as much pleasure to you, reading it, as it has to us writing it.

Publishing history: Keeping the Ocean Magical 2020. Poem 'Rejoice', Spiritual World Magazine 2015.

Brenda M Moss

I have written poetry and prose since childhood. I joined Mermaids several years ago, following meeting Susan on an Access to Higher Education, Creative writing module. Mermaids have helped me to critique my own work and that of sister Mermaids. The friendship and encouragement of Mermaid membership allow me to explore my inner voice and satisfy my hunger to share my thoughts. We are encouraged to enter our work to a wider audience, and we regularly enjoy listening to published authors. I am hoping to publish a family book on hop-picking soon, and a memoir of life as a child growing up in Medway.

Publishing history. Poem: Ultimate Colour Prejudice, River, Medway Adult Learning publication 2001. Short story:Our Seasalter Holiday, 84 Stories, 2019

Jayne Curtis

I am currently editing *Agent Allison*, an FBI series based in Chicago, USA. When I took a break from writing to look after my mother, the story continued to develop in outline form into a full series. This time also enabled the development of a spin-off story, *The Law Woman*, which is based on Agent Allison's Great, Great, Great Grandmother, in an 1860s Western. I find that action thrillers are great fun to write, and this kept me focused through lockdown. I'm looking forward to Agent Allison being published in 2023. Let the mayhem begin

Publishing history: Short Story: Hearing Aid, 84 Stories, 2019.

Angela Johnson

I grew up in West Wales, in a Welsh-speaking family, and the language of my childhood and the stories I heard inspired my novel *Arianwen* published by Black Bee Books. I became an English teacher, and later studied Creative Writing at the University of Kent and was awarded a Distinction. My novel *Harriet and her Women* was shortlisted for the Impress Prize for Fiction. My short story *George and the Dragon* was shortlisted for the H.E.Bates Memorial Short Story Prize. I won the Poetry Prize at the Folkestone Arts Festival for a poem in praise of older women. I am inspired by my interest in environmental causes, the beauty of the natural world and the infinite complexity of human nature. I feel impelled to write, as a way of giving meaning to the world. I enjoy the myriad possibilities of language. Importantly, I enjoy stories, creating them and reading them. Stories are nourishment for the soul. Belonging to a supportive, friendly group such as Medway Mermaids sustains me as a writer. Writing is a solitary occupation and listening to other writers is inspirational and enlightening.

Debra Frayne

I found Medway Mermaids back in 2015 and I am so glad that I did. As a mother to two young children, it was hard to find time to do things for myself, but right from the start, it felt like a home from home. The Mermaids are kind, patient, inspiring and encouraging and have a wealth of life experience and advice to give when it comes to writing. I aspire to write more in the future as my children grow up and need me less. I look forward to sharing more work with the rest of the group.

Judith Northwood-Boorman

Being a member of Medway Mermaids for 12 years has been fundamental to my writing journey. I would never have explored so many writing projects, including so many poetic forms, from haiku to limericks. Guest speakers like Fiona Sinclair, have been a revelation and inspiration. Being a Mermaid has improved both my style and confidence to enter competitions. As a result, I have had a poem in a national anthology, I was also the winner of the 2019 Westgate on Sea Literary Festival short story competition. My story *The Dream House* appears in my recently published collection: *Joie de Vivre* available from Feedaread.com. Other published books by HRG were used for fundraising purposes, raising almost £20,000: *Other publishing history: Georgia's Fantastic Christmas' 1996, 'Georgia's Fantastic Christmas and other stories' 2009. Happy Christmas Passengers, 84 Stories, 2019.*

Katrina Megget

I'm a freelance journalist writing about healthcare and medical science, as well as adventure travel and mental well-being for various trade and mainstream publications. I'm currently writing a book about my adventure walking the 3,000km (1,864 miles) Te Araroa Trail down the length of New Zealand. I also hope to write something on my most recent adventure sailing 2,000 miles clockwise around the coast of Great Britain with my partner Mark on a "cosy" 28-foot boat named Speedwell while raising funds for the UK charity SafeLives, which works to end domestic abuse. This is a cause close to my heart having experienced emotional abuse first-hand in a previous relationship. Originally from New Zealand, I now live in Gravesend with Mark. For more about me visit my website: (www.katrinamegget.com) ,
Public Facebook page (www.facebook.com/KatMegget/),
Twitter (https://twitter.com/katrinamegget),
Instagram (www.instagram.com/katrinamegget).

Catriona Murfitt

My relationship with words has not always been an easy one, as being dyslexic, autistic and ADHD made our relationship rocky in the early years. I loved to make up stories and create fantasy worlds more than I loved to read them. But when words started to make more sense, books became a portal for me away from the everyday world, which I sometimes struggled with, into worlds of adventure, magic, and wisdom. I love to read fantasy, and sci-fi, about impossible things or possible futures. I am fascinated by folklore particularly faerie lore, and the superstitious minds of those that came before. So, my writing reflects my love of the superstitious and fantastic. I write poetry and prose as a way of expelling demons or creating a snippet of unreality. I am currently working on two novels one based on folklore, the other a mix of fantasy and sci-fi.

Since joining Medway Mermaids, I have made new friends and we share our love of creative writing. The women of this group have kindly shared their life experiences, and the inspiration and guidance they provide has completely enhanced my writing. I will be forever grateful for this. When not lost in other worlds, I home-educate my three children. This has enriched my life and inspired me to be creative in all aspects of our lives. Home education gives me the opportunity to let my children explore the world at their pace and allows so much more time to adventure this life together.

Publishing history: Short Story: She Left, 84 Stories 2019.

Jackie Anderson

I have been a freelance writer for some years now, contributing articles to numerous online and print publications on issues as diverse as women's health, parenting, art and culture, business, and technology. I also write fiction and poetry, have published collections of poetry and a short story anthology, and have tutored writing workshops. I am based in Gibraltar where I have won awards for my writing and was part of the publishing team of the *Anthology of Gibraltar Poets* published in 2019. I frequently spend time with my family in Medway where I lived for many years. My favourite place in the world is somewhere deep inside a story.

Publishing history: Myth Monster Murderer - Jack the Ripper: the victims, the crimes, the story. 2022. All they Want for Christmas, Collection of Short Stories, 2020. Anthology of Contemporary Gibraltar Poets, 2019. The Last Lullaby: Chilling Stories for Winter Nights, 2018. Mind Me Please, Anthology of works on mental illness, Ed. Christian Rocca, 2017. Of Love and Shadows, Collection of poems, 2014.
Love Letters I Never Mailed, Anthology of poetry and stories, Editor Sonia Golt, 2011.

Guest Writers featured in this anthology.

These contributors are occasional members and friends of the group.

Kate Young
I have been writing poetry since childhood and belong to two active poetry groups. My poems have appeared in various webzines/magazines nationally and in Canada. It has also been featured in the anthologies *Places of Poetry* and *Write Out Loud*. My pamphlet *A Spark in the Darkness* is out now, published with Hedgehog Press. Find me on Twitter @Kateyoung12poet.

Kira Grayly
Discovering Medway Mermaids Ladies Writing Group when I first moved to Kent, I was overwhelmed by the friendliness with which I was received. I had often thought about writing but, with the busyness of life, had never put pen to paper. I was encouraged to try out every genre and felt very drawn to poetry as a way of self-expression. I would like to thank Sue for her patience and care in the development of my writing aspirations and the group for their kind and helpful suggestions and for sharing their knowledge with me.

Randa Saab
I was a member of The Mermaids for a few months three years ago before travelling to pursue my Art studies. I like to write in English and in Arabic, in prose and in poetry about spiritual exploration, human relationships, and women-related issues. I have a small collection of English poetry *On the Boat, the Voices of Refugees*, published on Amazon kindle. I have also written a novella in English about spiritual exploration, and an Arabic book about women in the Middle East. Both books are still waiting for a publisher. In September 2022, I have a solo art exhibition at the Halpern Gallery, Chatham, *Entitled: Two Years in Confinement.*

Stella Lambert
Just having a new pen inspires me. A notepad is always by my chair for random ideas about my next escapade! So many ideas, from putting the world to rights to fairy tales, written for friends, or for shouting out loud. I'm also an artist and love to combine art and words. I'm waiting for my next blank canvas to fill with poems, stories, and memories of yesteryear.

Lin Tidy

I began writing in 1980 when a Creative Writing class was mandatory at the US college I was attending. I discovered a love for it. I wandered into the Medway Mermaids in about 2012, having just completed my first book. I found a supportive, friendly and inspiring group of women. They unfailingly encouraged each other, whether that person had been writing for years or was just, tentatively dipping her toe. I write non-fiction generally, much of it coming under the heading of 'Social History.' I also write the occasional poem.

Publishing history: The Warrior on the Wall, 201., The Unsent Letter, 201. Harry and Bob, 2015. The Paper it's Written on, 2016. The Day We Buried The Fish, 2017.

Prologue Poem

The Siren's Whisper

Catriona Murfitt

Would you come with me?
Would you leave it all behind?
No more physical pain, no mental torment
No more disability shackling you.
Freedom of mind, body, and soul await.
Swim in a well of magic
Of power unyielding
No responsibilities
Just hedonistic pleasure.
No more worries, for they remain on this dry broken land,
Your wildest dreams touch only the surface of what I offer you.
Let go of your burden
It's okay,
Your children have their own stories to write,
Lives to live.
Your sacrifice means freedom,
Adventure unparalleled.
Would you come with me?
Leave it all behind?

Part One - MERMAID SONGS

Mermaids are strong independent women who lift their voices and want to be heard.

Mermaid's Song	Angela Johnson
Boats at Bay	Jackie Anderson
The Lost Mermaid	Brenda M Moss
Mermaid	Judith Northwood Boorman
The Girl by the Rock Pool	Katrina Megget
Be Like Sand	Catriona Murfitt
The Sea Horse	Susan Pope
Nanny Em	Judith Northwood Boorman
The Curious Mermaid	Debra Frayne
The Mermaids of Barrican Beach	Brenda M Moss
A Christmas Tale	Judith Northwood Boorman
The Mermaid's Kiss	Catriona Murfitt
Magical Ocean	Michele Barton Macintosh
A Mermaid with a Question	Judith Northwood-Boorman
Who am I?	Susan Pope
Liquid Blue	Jayne Curtis
Leap Frog	Ann Smith
The Changeling	Catriona Murfitt
The Waterfall	Nilufar Imam
The Lizard Lady of Lobos	Judith Northwood Boorman
River Runs Home	Kira Grayly
One Small Stone	Kate Young
Meeting The River 1992	Lin Tidy

Mermaid's Song

Angela Johnson

On a beach at the end of the earth,
I heard the mermaid sing.
Cold and jewelled night
Of cold and stars.
A collision of worlds
In the sadness of her song.
The moon slid cold into the sea,
She reached for its light:
Cold heartless moon.
The mermaid mourns,
Time is cruel,
Time is slow,
And she cursed to live
Each stretched second
Till the world ends.
She is the lamentations
Of History,
Encapsulation of loss,
Of yearnings,
Of incalculable mournings.

She calls me now,
My siren of the sea,
To its ice sculptured waves
And her world of mystery.

Boats at Bay

Jackie Anderson

They bob, a row of coloured corks,
Dipping first their prows
Then raising them again
To sniff at morning air,
Restless now the tide creeps in.
Tugging at their tethers
Like frothing colts
Eager to race out to sea,
To join the shoals,
To ride the streaming currents
That pluck at them now,
Hither, thither and thereabout.
Barnacled bows are tossed free of surf,
Bloated hulls, squat and round,
Shuffle and bustle and shove at each other,
Sterns swaying like the hips
Of plump young wives
On Beltane Eve, sipping ale,
And dancing sunset jigs.
They are at play, those little boats,
Held with hemp to wooden posts
At the shore of sheltered cove,
Where only ripples slap
Their sun-frayed sides.
Today at least, just children to the might
Of lordly fishing fleet
That braves the rougher waves
And dares to test the challenges
Of the dark, mysterious deep.

The Lost Mermaid

Brenda M Moss

I swim as gently as a shoal
of jellyfish on the move,
undulating, I cannot see,
Medway's mud is blinding me.

Resting on rocks, here I lie,
'Land ho, skipper'
goes up the cry,
jolly sailors shanty by.

I move along, for all to see,
beside the dock, beneath the sea,
undulating, undulating,
oh so, oh so, enticingly.

Enter, enter, enter me,
sing and cry and sigh with me,
swim and hold and set me free,
oh so, oh so, lovingly.

Crafts of every shape and size,
dwarf my tail, fins and eyes,
relentlessly, the crafts abound,
stretching onwards, to the Sound.

Beside the dock,
beneath the sea,
I move along,
enticingly.

A monstrous craft pulsating by,
is dragging me within its eye,
twisting, turning,
chokingly.

Beside the dock,
beneath the sea,
Resisting, persisting,
painfully.

A fisherman's hook,
lifts me high,
and leaves me gasping,
in the sky.

Gentle hands,
unhook my tail, will mortal man
hear my wail?
Against my will,
I lay here still, for all to see,
cruelly injured,
bloodily.

All pleasure gone,
worryingly,
beside the dock,
beneath the sea,
despair, despair,
despairingly.

As morning breeze,
gently tease,
sighing, crying,
lying still, resisting,
against my will.

Beside the dock,
now out to sea,
under, under,
undulatingly.

I swim as swiftly as I can,
and leave behind, this foreign land,
of flounder, eel, and
large sea bass,
seek parrot fish,
and rainbow wrasse.

With arms outstretched,
I know that I,
can call on Scylla
and hear her sigh.

Terror's still
engulfing me,
my tail is weak,
I cannot see,
arching, bleeding,
painfully.

Beside the dock,
now out to sea,
ever onwards, wait for me,
I'm coming home,
Tyrrhenian Sea.

Mermaid

Judith Northwood Boorman

I wish I was a Mermaid
Swimming in the sea

I wish I was a mermaid
Then I would be free

I wish I was a mermaid
Basking on the rocks

I wish I was a mermaid
Not wearing any socks

I wish I was a mermaid
Pearls in my hair

I wish I was a mermaid
Without human care

I wish I was a mermaid
With an emerald tail

I wish I was a mermaid
Diamonds glittering on every scale

I wish I was a mermaid
Swimming with the whales

I wish I was on a desert island
Writing lots of mermaid tales.

The Girl by the Rock Pool

Katrina Megget

The old man watched her from behind the rock.

Goodness, she is beautiful.

Her hair dazzled like a thousand sunsets, her skin the finest porcelain ever made. When she laughed, it sounded like summer, and oh, how her eyes twinkled.

She trailed her fingertips in the waters of the rock pool, teasing the guppies and starfish.

The old man shifted for a better view. Mesmerised.

His sandals on the gravel startled her. She flinched and froze. Then, with a flick of her hair, dove into the surf, her rainbow tail shimmering until the dark waters welcomed her.

The old man stroked his beard. "Yes, what a magnificent creature I created."

Be like sand...

Catriona Murffit

Anger is like a rock thrown into a calm sea.
It makes ripples, it has an effect.
It has caused its anger to spread, it has caused unrest, worry and hate.
Its ripples will become a wave, the wave a tsunami; angry and rushing
without thought, without reason set on a path of destruction.
Anger becomes hate, hate becomes blame, blame becomes revenge,
revenge becomes hurt, hurt becomes fear,
and fear becomes anger and on and on it goes,
wave after crashing devastating wave,
bringing nothing but ruin and despair.
So when the tide goes back out,
the landscape may have changed,
it may have swept away more than is right or just.
But then the choice is ours.
Do we pick up rocks to throw our upset, our anger, our hurt,
back at the vast sea?
Do we send out more ripples of hate in a never-ending cycle?
Ripple after ripple
Wave after wave
Destruction, death, and devastation
on constant violent repeat?
Or do we stand together?
Rebuild, reunite?
We are mightier in our union.
We will not harden our hearts to stone.
We will not become of rock.
Rather let us be like sand,
let each individual grain, diverse and unique in its nature
come together in peaceful force.
That angry jagged rock will be made smooth in our presence,
it will lose its cutting edge.
It's power made redundant by its inability to divide us.

There is more good than evil in this world.
Together with time we can make that small piece of rock erode to dust.
The waters will calm.
The ripples will cease
That anger that was will be but a drop in the ocean.
One bad stone
Just a pebble…
The earth is too full of wonder and love, don't let one pebble blind you.
Don't hold it in your hand like a worry stone to wear you down,
to steal you of your hope, to take away your joy.
Discard that stone filled with fear into the water.
Cast it away and
let it drown.
Be kind to yourself and others
Let your ripples be of love
Let your waves be compassion
Let peace come back to the sea.

The Sea Horse

Susan Pope

Why did I not evolve as others did?
Grow legs, diversify, become amphibious?
Crawl from the safety of our watery home
Walk across the sand, a creature of the land.
They galloped on through evolution
As flying dragons and powerful drays.
Unwilling partners in man's destiny,
They returned, shimmering stallions, rearing and foaming,
Translucent white chargers topping the waves,
Diving down to our undersea caves.
While I remained unchanged, male and female,
A question mark, a beginning without end.

Nanny Em

Judith Northwood Boorman

Our Nanny Em is very special. She is not like most other nannies. She can't run around with us, but we do have fun on her mobility scooter when she gives us a ride. She also plays tag with us. She normally wins, as her scooter goes faster than we can run. She is always cheerful and happy despite her disability. We don't know when it happened, but she lost the use of her legs a long time ago. She doesn't like to talk about it.

She always keeps her legs covered up with a blanket. But she does like to go swimming in the sea but because she does not like anyone to see her legs she won't swim with other people. We don't live very near the sea so the local swimming pool has a special arrangement for Nanny Em. She goes swimming every day at 5:30 before the rest of the swimmers arrive at 6:30. I've never known her to miss one day swimming. She even goes on Christmas Day. She knows the manager of the leisure centre very well and he comes and opens up especially for her.

But, one day, she let us go with her to the seaside. Normally it's just Mummy. It seemed quite a palaver for Nanny to get changed. She has this enormous tent that covers her mobility scooter so that she can get undressed in private. What we didn't know was that her mobility scooter could actually go in the water too.

Then with a big splash Nanny Em was off. What a spectacular swimmer. She can hold her breath for an amazing amount of time, and she doesn't need goggles over her eyes. Both my brother and I can't bear water in our eyes. Particularly not salt water.

'Please can we swim with Nanny Em' we pleaded with Mum.

'No, it's too dangerous' replied Mum.

'Why?' I questioned. 'Surely Nanny Em can keep an eye on us?'

'No, that's the problem. She can't. Once she's in the water she forgets all her limitations. It will be too deep for you.'

It just didn't make sense to me.

Not until I was a lot older and had a bike. I got up very early and went to the leisure centre. There are huge plate glass windows where you can see the pool from outside the building.

What a shock I had.

I was expecting to see Nanny Em's damaged legs. Instead of that she was skimming through the water like a giant fish. A magnificent powerful tail, with its iridescent green, silver, and blue scales, skimming through the pool's clear water.

It all became clear. Em wasn't the short form of Emma, as we'd always believed, but M for Mermaid.

We are so fortunate to have not only a Nanny, but our very own Nanny Mermaid! A fact we will have to keep top secret.

'Nanny M, your secret's safe with me.' I whispered to myself as I cycled home for breakfast.

The Curious Mermaid

Debra Frayne

Rough waves slapped the rocks.

Surveying green eyes peered up and webbed fingers reached for a better grip before lifting her slender form from the ocean's embrace.

The biting wind was chilling but she had to do this! Her mission burned inside her, keeping her resolve intact. She was lithe and swift in her element, but awkward and heavy without.

It took all her strength to pull herself across to the nest. A screech sounded and she waved off the angry mother bird. She smiled down in wonder at the tiny chicks.

So that's what baby gulls look like.

The Mermaids of Barrican Beach

Brenda M Moss

It had been a sunny day on the beach, with a blue sky, hardly any clouds and a gentle breeze.

The holidaymakers had all left, traipsing home for their tea, but leaving behind their litter. A small group of volunteers were walking along the beach, with black sacks and pincer grippers, picking up the beer cans, sandwich wrappers, lollipop sticks and leftover food scraps. Amongst it all, the seagulls screeched above, diving down amidst the volunteers, calling to one another, in their attempts to snatch away something edible.

Out at sea, the mermaids were all circling, marshalling the herring towards the dolphins, who always helped them to herd the catch of the day. They traditionally worked together. It was for the common good.

At the head of the formation, Sargassum, the older chief mermaid, clicked and clucked at her companions. In return, the dolphins squeaked back at her. She could see that young Kelp and Algae were working hard, but Samphire had lagged behind and she knew that she would have to break away and swim behind her, to move things along.

'Come on Samphire, get a move on,' ordered Sargassum through a long stream of bubbles. She could see that Samphire did not have her heart in it at all. Sargassum had noticed that Samphire had been growing larger recently and it was making her move much more slowly in the water. She seemed to be unhappy too, about something as she swam along, her head down, gazing at the seabed and not ahead as she should be.

Sargassum caught up with Samphire and blew a large stream of pink bubbles into her face. Samphire responded immediately and with a flip of her turquoise tail, continued to herd the herring towards the dolphins. Sargassum swam alongside Samphire.

'I want to see you in my cave after the drive. We need to discuss what is

31

going on with you.' She spoke through minute pink bubbles, as Samphire gazed back defiantly at her. The younger mermaid formed her arms into an acknowledgement arc above her hair. She knew what was wrong with her, but she did not want to discuss it with Sargassum. No. Not with anyone really. But of course, she had to. With a strong flip of her golden tail, Sargassum beat her way forward, leaving a trail of golden pink-coloured bubbles behind her.

Kelp and Algae swam vigorously ahead of Samphire, green bubbles surrounding them both and then circled back around her, swooping and diving, turning somersaults and laughing at one another, as they drove the straggling herring towards the dolphins. They would soon all finish for the day and head for their caves amongst the rocks. Samphire knew that Kelp and Algae would start their primping, eyelash fluttering and descaling of their tails and fins. She also knew that they were probably meeting up with Neptune later. If his minder, Salacia, was to discover what they were all up to, she would have a hissy fit. Samphire knew a lot about the other mermaids, but she kept quiet. Everyone trusted her to be discreet. She was the nursery's mermaid. All the new babies were in her care. She could see them now, on the seabed, being looked after by Baltic Tellin, the wise giant-sized seahorse. He was always happy to look after the babies when Samphire was needed for the daily herring drive.

Samphire was miserable. She would have liked to have had some baby mermaids of her own, but all she seemed to do, was to look after the other mermaid's babies. Every year, she got more bloated, until now, finally, she felt that she needed to pop, but she knew that would not happen on its own. She needed to be gently shaken by Neptune and pricked on her bottom with his three-pronged black trident. His eyes never rested on her. She felt completely overlooked, full of possible future babies but no-one to shake and pop her.

This is what she needed explain to Sargassum. Later, in the luminous, shell covered walls, of her cave, Sargassum nodded wisely, as Samphire explained. She had heard it all before.

'I cannot decide who is next to pop, you know that Samphire. If Neptune does not point his trident at you and overlooks you again this season, I cannot intervene. You could try fluttering your eyelids at his brother Jupiter, but whatever you do, do not let his minder Juno catch you out. If she does, she will have you sent off to the shark lower levels, to be eaten.'

Samphire shook her head. 'I am the nursery Mermaid, Sargussum, surely, I am protected from Juno's jealous rages?'

'Only until the end of this season, Samphire. After that, well I am afraid you are on your own. We may even have to elect another nursery Mermaid, especially as you have grown so large. No telling when you might explode and who would look after all the mermaid babies then, with you in pieces, all over the seabed?' Samphire nodded, even more upset. What was she to do?

Samphire was desperate, so she asked Baltic Tellin if he could look after the creche, over the next sunrise or two. She had made up her mind. She was going to seek out Jupiter. There was no point waiting for Neptune. He was just not interested in pointing his trident at her at all. She was determined to have her popping season before she exploded. Why shouldn't she be like all the other mermaids? It just didn't seem fair. It had to be this season. It was now, or never, Samphire decided.

It was getting dark, Moonlight shimmered on the top of the waves and Samphire swayed, patiently waiting, hidden away in the long grass fronds and rocks around the entrance to Jupiter's cave. Suddenly, a loud trumpeting sound came towards her, out of the darkness and riding on the back of a giant shark, was Jupiter.

'He is handsome,' realised Samphire, noticing his golden hair and beard and strong arms as he held the bridle in his left hand, and with his right, he cut at the long grass, with a huge shining silver blade, not a black trident. He sensed a mermaid, and blew out red bubbles as he moved down to where Samphire was waiting and hiding.

'Ahh, a mermaid, at last,' Jupiter bellowed, and in the half-light, Samphire floated gently up and alongside Jupiter and nuzzled her face around his cheeks and chin. Jupiter's eyes glinted. He reached for Samphire and pulled her by the hand towards his chest. He kept pulling her, to and fro holding both hands, until Samphire, singing loudly, expelled yellow bubbles from her mouth. As Jupiter pushed and pulled Samphire's body against his, suddenly, she felt a huge pop in her tail, where her tiny secret cave was, and hundreds of tiny babies, inside large green bubbles, drifted up and away, lost in the clouds of coral spores, everywhere around them. The large seahorse, Baltic Tellin, saw all the action taking place and rushed to gather up all the bubbles, fanning his fins at them in an attempt to brush the green bubbles containing the tiny babies, down into the large nursery shell lying open on the ocean floor.

'At last,' Samphire exclaimed, as she spun around and around, making her way up towards the moonlight on the top of the waves.

'I have finally popped,' she shouted with her head out of the water, and she swam away excitedly, a lot slimmer than the day before. Jupiter steered the shark along the seabed, then he rushed to the surface, too, did a high jump up into the air and splashed back down again, diving under the waves, happy to have fathered more babies, instead of his brother Neptune.

The following sunset, there were a lot more babies in the creche sleeping. Their bubbles had all melted and they floated gently around, inside the large seashell, amongst the pearls, together with their older mermaid cousins. Samphire, seemed to have more energy now that she had popped so successfully and she swam above the babies, fanning them with her long turquoise tail.

At the next herring drive, suddenly, a mermaid the size of a human female, swam alongside Samphire and smacked her tail against the side of Samphire's body, knocking her sideways.

'I am Juno. I have been told that you have been popping with Jupiter. Is that correct?'

What could Samphire say? She had of course, but should she admit it? Would Juno have her sent off to the shark's lower levels, to be eaten?

'I have been growing larger for a long time,' said Samphire. 'I needed popping, or I was going to burst all over the seabed. Jupiter helped me to pop, and for that I am very grateful.' Juno nodded her head, causing her mauve hair to weave around her, in dramatic swirling movements.

'I approve. It was necessary because you are the nursery mermaid. None of us could manage our daily lives, without you in attendance in the nursery all day.'

Samphire smiled at Juno, with gratitude, and with a beat of her fine scaly silver tail, Juno swam away. As Samphire swam alongside Kelp and Algae, she knew that she would now be able to keep up with all the beautiful slim mermaids in future. She would not have to worry about popping ever again, and she gazed down at the large seashell on the seabed, holding her own tiny baby mermaids.

The Mermaid's Kiss

Catriona Murfitt

Her silver tongue
Sang lyrical
With voice
Conjured images erotic in his mind
Her scales luminous reflecting both sun and sea
Felt flesh of legs that looked awkward in her ocean
Skin on scale
The water entwined the land
She pulled him to her world
His fingers tangled in sea green hair
She kissed rough warm lips inhaling air
He kissed soft cold lips inhaling the ocean
One more kiss and you may stay with me?
Her azure eyes whispered to his soul
He kissed her once more
His life consumed by the vast sea
As his soul drifted away.

A Christmas Tale

Judith Northwood Boorman

It's freezing as I creep out of the house as quietly as possible.

I hope I haven't woken the rest of my family with my early morning regime. It's become somewhat of an obsession. They think I'm mad. Climbing into my sparkling frost-encrusted car, I begin to think so too.

Joining the snaking buzz of dawn traffic, in minutes I'm in the car park adjacent to the River Medway. It's already cluttered with cars. No doubt at 6 am the other fanatics have queued beneath the hallowed green portal, awaiting its vast doors to be unlocked. Eager devotees scurried to worship at their mechanical altars. Their new god: the body beautiful.

In contrast, I hobble through the reception area. The obligatory twinkling Christmas tree seemingly nods at me, surrounded by alluring, sparkly wrapped (but empty) gift boxes.

No muscle-pumping machines for me! The pool beckons. Within minutes, I am slipping into its heavenly embrace. Goggles in place, I dive beneath the deliciously warm water for my daily baptism.

Swimming as far as possible on one breath of air, pearl-like bubbles escape from my lips. Beneath me, the glittering blue mosaic tiles resemble a stained-glass window. It's beautiful and this feels akin to a spiritual experience.

On my first length of the pool, I spot something glinting silver, caught in the filter grille beneath me. I gulp a lungful of air, diving down to investigate. It seems to be a small Christmas tree decoration. I pull, but it won't release. After many ineffectual tugs, I can't hold my breath any longer, I lunge to the surface, gasping like an overweight, oxygen-hungry porpoise. Unabashed, I suck another lungful of air and dive again.

I tug urgently at the silvery thread. This time, the grille comes away. A mass of grey swirling murky water snatches me in a vortex of fury, sucking me towards a black hole. I am thrashing and twisting in the grasp of a malign, surging force, spinning like a demonic top. My eyes bulge, my lungs screaming in silent prayer, but I can't resist the force of this bottomless abyss.

The darkness engulfing me starts to clear. I can see a green-tinged light flickering above me. My breathing is laboured but at least I'm breathing. The previous pressure in my lungs disperses through my ears in a myriad of tiny gyrating bead-like bubbles. I have a strange tingling in my legs, which increases to the intensity of a thousand stabbing knives. I look down at my once lily-white flabby legs. They have fused, now bonded into a peculiar shape: an iridescent, green scaly tail. One swish of my new powerful appendage, I burst to the surface. I'm in the cool waters of the river. On the bank opposite, the health club, emblazoned with Christmas fairy lights, winks at me benignly.

I have heard of the fabled Medway Mermaids. I never believed I would unwittingly join their ranks.

Yet there's just one vital question on my mind:

'Do mermaids have a Bluewater?' I hope so. I haven't finished my Christmas shopping yet!

Magical Ocean

Michele Barton Macintosh

A ripple, a splash, a wave upon the ocean,
A dolphin flipper, a bottle nose, seen in motion.
Something's causing a commotion,
Swimming side by side, a notion.

Hands break the surface, red hair, splatters upon the face,
Swipes her fringe from her eyes. What's taking place?
A human, swimming amongst dolphins? Something's displaced
Flip of turquoise, green and blue tail, glistening scales, ace!

Bubbles start to rise, they swim apart
Dolphin's tail flips, sadness upon its face, take heart,
A sigh escapes the mermaid's lips, they now depart.
Ariel has lost her love, a new life has to start.

A Mermaid with a Question

Judith Northwood Boorman

'Why am I here?'
Screeching noises from overhead shock her awake.
She is in a hammock.
Certainly not her normal domain.

Then she remembers.
A monstrous wave, the like of which she's never seen before,
violently tumbles her body onto shore,
like a piece of gnarled driftwood.

She claws at the waves in desperation.
Then panic-stricken, becomes entangled,
suffocating in a web of alien material.
Coarse and scratchy.

Now she has another question.
'How am I going to get back?'

Who am I?

Susan Pope

Cera sits on a stool, her legs crossed to one side. Her easel and paints are ready.

'Today, I must find my true self.'

She paints the top half of her naked body. It is always the legs which cause her problems.

She empties her mind, and her fingers find the blue pallet. She is mesmerised watching the brush arc down, spawning a fishtail.

She feels a surge of joy.

With deft strokes, she fills in the sky and sea in moody blues.

Cera slides from the stool into the wild wet waves.

With a flick of her tail – she disappears.

Liquid Blue

Jayne Curtis

Reflection of colours

Impress my eyes.

I stand

this bridge holds me

alone

In claustrophobic peace.

But I welcome it

Allured by dreams of

lavender and pink sorbet hues.

I dip my toe to wade

amongst the lily heads.

Leap Frog

Ann Smith

Spawning ritual complete,
Tadpoles swimming at my feet,
Head or tails, small and neat,
In my little pond

Mass invasion. fish in limbo,
Hide among weed and trim oh,
Croaking throats and legs akimbo,
In my little pond.

Exodus bodies jumping,
Bubble eyes hearts pumping,
Avoiding birds and cat that's lunching
In my little pond.

Next year cycle starts again,
Winters over then comes rain,
Fishy banquet eggs remain,
In my little pond.

The Changeling
Catriona Murfitt

My thoughts are rapid,
But my words come out slow.
Lightening trapped in treacle
In my mind I have traversed the world and spoken to gods
In that time in your world, I've only said three words.

I've watched for as long as I can remember,
Movements of hands, the nuance of lips
The sparks of individuality that build a human
I mirror in the mirror till I assimilate

In the light I smile and I speak
In the dark I fade away
In the light I recreate
In the dark I pine for a home
Still, I yearn to be a person of light,
But like a moth to a flame
My time in the sun burns me.

You don't understand me
Or I you.
My mind is not the same as yours
My view differs greatly
I see the threads that bind our worlds
But I have not the power to control or contort
I am stuck where I do not belong
Yet I look like you,
all flesh,
all bone
No, I am something different
See the world upside down
Or to the side
Not straight forward

Before I existed, you created an image
A human experience, a whole life
I'm sorry that life does not dwell in this form
You were tricked
By an ideal,
By normalcy,
By expectation
To you I am ill-formed
I am seen as disordered
But I have power within me
I have magic. If only you had true sight
You'd see me shine.
I see the things you do not
I see the patterns that make up the universe.
I see so many details you take for granted.
What you see I also feel, smell and taste
Heightened sensory overload
Different neurology
A gift
A curse.

I am awkward, a spectacle
Emotionally unstable
Either numb or built of raw emotion
A volcano coldly dormant yet spilling lava
There is no in-between for me
Only extremes, all or nothing
I am both too much and not enough
I hear words of either, calm down
Or, there, she's off with the faeries again
Oh, if only you knew!
......
I do not fit
I'm an obtuse triangle forced through a circular hole
I am not whole but only because you can't see me

Are denied my true form
You see me as broken,
I see your world as broken
I do not belong here
Trapped in this ill-fitted body.
The reflection I see in your intrusive eyes
Is not my own.
My soul glimpses freedom in quiet spaces
Alas, nowhere is without sound.
Not in this noisy world full of noisy humans
Where my voice is scarcely heard
But I am here.

The Waterfall

Nilufar Imam

A mere child was I, staring endlessly at the cloud in the sky
Wondering how such soft floating fluff miraculously
Changed to water, lost its balance and fell?

I only saw little or big puddles after a rain fall.
Later learnt these become collections to form streams
Merging into rivers, the ocean being the destination of all.

Mysteriously, during the journey, an expanse of water tumbled
One or more steep drops, create the spectacular waterfall.
More amazingly, these might even be seen with dropping

Meltwater, over the edge of an ice-shelf, iceberg, or a glacier
What a splendid show of Mother Nature
Creating a sight so spectacular,
Of sprays and rainbows with such energy
Enthralling man with the sound and colour.

Footnote:
First published in Searching for the Rainbow, Nilufar Imam 2022

The Lizard Lady of Lobos

Judith Northwood Boorman

She lives amongst the rocks and sand,
In this hostile barren land.
The seals have fled some years ago,
This Islet made by lava flow.
She swirls around in leopard prints,
Sharing with tourists, tips and hints
And pointing out her numerous pals:
The lizards living in the vales
Of volcanic rock, or beneath the plants
which in the wind gyrate and dance.
She feeds the lizards crumbs of bread,
Ensuring they are all well fed.
The lizards love her, everyone
Basking in the fierce hot sun.

River Runs Home

Kira G. Grayly

Where am I?
Pushing myself through, onto the peaty Earth,
I inhale its warmth and shake out my tumbling curls.
Experiencing my newfound voice I gurgle with laughter
Rejoicing at my birth, curiosity pushing me forward.
Little by little I grow and flow a little faster as I play,
bubbling over the slippery rocks
Head-over-heeling into the golden pebble bed
Green weed tickling my tummy and fish-lets kissing my toes.

Who is that hiding in the reeds?
Another to play with! "Come play with me," I call, waving -
Running you come to the edge and say,
"Where are we going and what will we find?"
You jump in – we laugh and play, curiosity pushing us ever forward.
Then suddenly - you disappear – I lose sight of you
 at the place of the dark burial mound,
And I am left to travel on alone. I grow… alone,
Sometimes I leave my journeying to sit beneath a willow tree
I kneel, head bent, hair weeping into the river.

Who are they?
They skim past, I dive back in, to join their winding forms,
Arms forward, hair of emerald-green flowing back.
"Wait," I splutter, skimming round obstacles
Tearing myself in two as I try to decide which direction to follow,
Into three, four, five parallel tributaries.
The flowing continues ever faster
Till, my divided soul unites again.
I have matured, I am strong, look at my girth.

How I have grown, so much water flows behind me now
And look! On the horizon I can see the sea,
How fast was my journeying?
Can it be over so soon?
"Hey, Over Here!" I shout and wave as all the rivers I have ever known
or met
Join with me now at this one place
And together
We rush towards that Vast Ocean
Becoming One Singular Wave of curiosity.

"Again, again!"
We call out laughing.

One Small Stone

Kate Young

Eight years old, skimming stones
across a lake made of foil,
enjoying the rub of pebble in palm.

I watched the water shiver
excited by precision,
your elbow angled perfectly.

My turn, more lob than scud,
I recall the stone-echo as it sunk
heavy as disappointment.

You demonstrated carefully,
a honed technique to
tickle the glaze with dimples.

I was transfixed.
How could one small stone
cause such an effect?

Actions have consequences
you explained, *we all live*
in the wake of ripple-spill.

Meeting the River – 1992

Lin Tidy

It was February when
the river came to meet her
at the bridge
blind date clothed
in its winter brown

she'd left behind a life
she'd failed to live
in a treeless place
no features to recall
or long for
just the ordered
fields, worked
until they dropped
But the river is where
she would begin

like so many times before
she would make
friends
and enemies
and hardly see the difference

she would
come to know,
that the river would always
keep its secrets
and she would have
no need to understand

Part Two   **MERMAID TEARS**

Part Two contains more profound pieces, some reflecting members'
concerns for our world, and some of the tragedies unfolding around us.
Others are pure fiction.

Earth's Children

Kira G Grayly

Fukushima Disaster - 11 March 2011

It's been four years since we saw home,
Ghost town, in the exclusion zone,
And the vision haunts us still -
When first we felt the power of Earth,
Open up the peaceful sea,
Tremorous alarm, of the approaching
Tsunami.

Gaia sent Poseidon
Death personified
Raging from the depth
Towering, arms outstretched
Between us, and the sun and sky
Obscuring the horizon's boundary
Then dark, unswerving line
Of water, bodies, cars, and homes
Came crashing down -
On Fukushima town.

It was an act of stealth
That Nature did employ

Her conscious intervention and intent
to prevent us from meddling
with her atoms and elements.

Mother's reprimand, palpable in our fearful minds
Then... with
wet fingertips growing, feeling, and flowing
Her target she found,
And She washed and melted all within,
And shut those reactors down

See footnote over page.

Footnote:
A stone tablet in Aneyoshi, Japan, warns residents not to build homes below it. Hundreds of these so-called tsunami stones, some more than six centuries old, dot the coast of Japan. (Credit Ko Sasaki for The New York Times)

Stone's translation:
"High dwellings are the peace and harmony of our descendants; remember the calamity of the great tsunami. Do not build any homes below this point."

ANEYOSHI, Japan — The stone tablet has stood on this forested hillside since before they were born, but the villagers have faithfully obeyed the stark warning carved on its weathered face: "Do not build your homes below this point!"

Residents say this injunction from their ancestors kept their tiny village of 11 households safely out of reach of the deadly tsunami last month that wiped out hundreds of miles of Japanese coast and rose to record heights near here. The waves stopped just 300 feet below the stone.

"They knew the horrors of tsunamis, so they erected that stone to warn us," said Tamishige Kimura, 64, the village leader of Aneyoshi.

Hundreds of so-called tsunami stones, some more than six centuries old, dot the coast of Japan, silent testimony to the past destruction that these lethal waves have frequented upon this earthquake-prone nation. But modern Japan, confident that advanced technology and higher seawalls would protect vulnerable areas, came to forget, or ignore these ancient warnings, dooming it to repeat bitter experiences when the recent tsunami struck.

From The New York Times 'Tsunami Warnings, Written in Stone, By MARTIN FACKLER APRIL 20, 2011.

Water Weed

Catriona Murfitt

The buzzing of mosquitoes brought a strange comfort. It was a familiar sound that Jenny recognised to be home. Odd to find comfort in what most found annoyance. She was not worried about the mosquitoes biting, as they seemed to mostly leave her alone. Unlike her mother who came out in huge welts and always questioned her decision to move to the salt marsh.

The two of them lived in a small cottage on the edge of a salt marsh in Lancashire. Jenny had never known anywhere but the marshlands. And didn't care too much to ever leave. Any excursion too far from home left her feeling quite drained. She despised the busyness of towns, so much rushing, so many faces, so many aromas, so many lights. They had only holidayed once when Jenny was barely old enough to remember. But her mother had said Jenny had come down with a bug and spent the entire time sick in bed. Her mother didn't take her too far from the marshes again, but Jenny didn't mind, she liked it here with her mosquitoes and wild birds.

Jenny was not your typical fourteen-year-old girl. She had been home educated and given the freedom of the marshes. She had no interest in the social groups for home-educated kids her mother had tried to get her involved with. Jenny preferred the sound of the wind rustling through the grass, the song of the birds and the hum of activity from all the creatures that dwelled in the marsh, rather than the sound of other, quite often, screaming children. So, where some girls her age might have been obsessing over pop bands and make-up, she much preferred to go pond dipping and record the migration of birds. Her mother, she remembered, used to try to keep her away from the marshes. Scared of her drowning in the pools, she had told Jenny that there were hidden dangers in wild places such as this. But Jenny could not be held back and her mother in the end gave up trying to stop her.

Jenny was looking out of the open kitchen window. It was the end of spring, and the sun was bringing more humidity to the land. She gazed longingly at her view of the swampy marshes ahead. She could see skylarks feeding in the long grass and the lapwings flying ahead. She wished to join them. Absent-minded, she swirled her fingers around in the water of the sink where she was meant to be washing the breakfast dishes. She liked the way the water moved around her fingers, enjoyed the feeling of it. She couldn't wait to get outside. She wanted to keep an eye out for the peregrine falcon she had seen. She was sure she had spotted it a few days ago, but it was a bit late in the season to be seeing them now and her curiosity was piqued.

"Water weed!" Came her mother's voice calling from the living room. Water weed being her mother's pet name for her for as long as she could remember. Her mother had always said her daughter would come back from the marshes more weed than human even as a small child.

"Yes, Mum," she called back

"Can you make me a coffee, love?" her mother's voice asked. She sounded tired and stressed. Her mum was an environmental writer, that's why she had come to live by the marshes. A publishing agent had shown interest in the book she was writing about salt marsh habitats and now she was under contract she had to work to deadlines. It was sad as her mother's fascination with this place was probably equal to Jenny's. But where Jenny seemed to thrive and breathe in this land, her mother stood outside of it observing from an academic point of view. She was always typing or taking photographs and was forever stressed. Jenny felt sorry for her, she worked so hard yet didn't get the pure enjoyment that Jenny did from exploring their home.

Jenny shook off the sink water from her hands and walked over to the percolator. There were no grounds in the metal basket or in the jar kept next to it. The spare grounds were on the top shelf in the cupboard. She opened the door and reached up, the tips of her fingers barely brushed the bottom of the box even on tip toes, she tried her best to reach a bit further. But then, there was a horrid painful cracking sound almost as if the bones in her outstretched arm were breaking. Unbelievably her arm seemed to be growing longer. Freaked out she quickly pulled her arm back down and rubbed it with the hand of her other arm, the pain quickly subsiding. She stretched both arms out in front her and Jenny was sure that one arm was longer than the other. But in the blink of an eye, it had shrunk so both her arms were equal in size.

Jenny ran to the front room where her mother was staring at the screen of her laptop concentrating, strain on her face.

"Mum, mum my arm grew!" she cried out.

Her mum looked up, both bemused and a bit irritated. "What on earth are you going on about?"

"My arm it grew. I was reaching for the coffee, and it grew!" Jenny implored.

Her mother sighed heavily but did look concerned. She got up and walked over to her daughter. "Hold your arms out."

"Well, they're the same size now," Jenny protested but held her arms out anyway.

Her mum held Jenny's hands aloft surveying her arms. "They are the same size, love but wow, Jenny your nails? When did you last cut them?"

Jenny looked at her nails. They were long, longer than they had grown before, but she wasn't hugely into self-care. Jenny shrugged, she was more upset about her mum brushing off the growing arm incident.

"It hurt, mum" Jenny pleaded.

"Probably growing pains. You're growing into a woman, my wonderful little water weed." She smiled looking up into Jenny's eyes. Suddenly her smile distorted into disgust, or was it fear? "Jenny, have you brushed your teeth this morning?"

"Yeah," Jenny said scratching her tooth with her fingernail. She looked down at her finger and there under her nail was a green substance.

"You need to brush them again, they look green." Jenny's mum hesitated, that strange, frightened look still showing on her face. She quickly added, "and you're not going to go out to the marshes. I need your help with something here today!"

The change in tone in her mother's voice and her obvious panic confused Jenny. It had been a long time since she had been told she couldn't go out. And why would dirty teeth trigger mum to act like this?

"Why? Surely, I can go out after we're done doing whatever you need help with?" Jenny countered.

"No, you are staying in today, all day, and tomorrow too!" Her mother's voice sounded frustrated, almost angry.

"What!" Jenny started to respond.

"Don't argue with me, young lady, now go and brush your teeth," her mother said, then she turned away to show she was not going to say anything else on the matter.

Jenny turned on her heels and stalked up the stairs to the bathroom.
What's up with mum today? she thought, I know she's stressed but to take it out on me so much, why?

She angrily grabbed her toothbrush and added too much paste to spite her mother, who hated waste. She bared her teeth at the mirror. They were very green, they looked grass stained. Jenny couldn't figure out why. She'd had baked beans for breakfast, and they wouldn't stain teeth green! With a little effort though, the green came off. She put down her toothbrush and grabbed the nail clippers out of the bathroom cupboard and sat on the shut toilet. Her nails were very long. She snipped, with some effort, each one down to a sensible length. Then she put both of her arms out in front of her again, still the same size.

She decided maybe her mum was right, a simple case of growing pains. Maybe Jenny just imagined the growing bit because it hurt? But she still felt it was unfair how quickly her mum got cross with her. So what if her teeth were dirty, hardly the end of the world, was it?

No good staying mad. Maybe if I help her out she will change her mind and let me go out; play it sweet.

Jenny shook her body as if to shake away her moodiness and set a smile on her face. She walked down the hall and hopped down the stairs back into the living room. On entering she saw her mum back behind her desk, coffee in hand, looking worried.

"You okay, mum?" she said, truly a little concerned.

Jenny's mum looked up, her face full of complex fearful emotion, but there was also determination in her eyes.

"Jenny..." she began, but then the determination instantly faded to be replaced by worry as she stumbled over her next words. "Yeah, I..I'm fine, s..sorry ... I'm strung out with this research and that's not your fault," her mum said instead.

"So, what do you want me to help with?" Jenny wanted to get straight to it. The sooner she was done helping her mum the sooner she would have her freedom.

"Oh... yeah... erm.. ." Jenny's mum looked like she was searching her brain for something to say.

"So, really important stuff then." Jenny couldn't help herself

"Jenny," her mum admonished

"Sorry." Jenny instantly backpedalled.

"That's fine, love, what I need you to do is categorise my photos into land, water and sky images." Her mum honestly looked like she had plucked the idea out of the air in front of her.

Jenny didn't really think this was something her mother needed her to do, but in hopes of keeping her happy so the rest of the day could be hers, she played along.

She walked over to the grey metal filing cabinet where her mum kept her research and photographs and pulled out the relevant folders. She was sure her mum had already made digital copies of all these photos and had them categorised, in groups a little more complex than land, water and sky. But she diligently went to the coffee table and started to order the photographs into the three categories. At least the pictures were of things she loved. It could have been worse.

The job of categorising the photographs was not as simple as Jenny had previously thought. Most of the pictures had all three elements in them.

After a bit of huffing and puffing, she decided she would divide them into mostly land, mostly water and mostly sky piles, with a fourth pile made up of the pictures where all three elements took equal place. Now she had a system it was a lot easier for her to get on with.

The room was quiet, all Jenny could hear was the tapping of her mother's fingers on the keyboard, the oddly recognisable peewit of the lapwings flying over the marshes and the shuffling of photos in her hands.

All of a sudden, the peaceful quiet became distorted and muffled. Jenny felt as if her head had become submerged below water. The tapping of her mother's fingers, and the bird song, became echoed and muted. She could hear the sound of water so distinctly. Together with the sound of air bubbles rippling, searching for freedom and a swooshing repetitive noise like the tide. Disoriented she looked around, her vision became fogged again, like trying to look through water. She felt her breath becoming more rapid. She tried to get up but knocked into the coffee table. Then she saw her mother's worried face appear in front of her.

"Jenny, are you okay?" Her mother's words were muffled.

"I... I don't know what's happening, mum, I can't see or hear properly." Jenny could feel her own tears rolling down her face.

"It's going to be okay, Jenny, just breathe in slowly and out again, like we did when we last went into town, remember." Jenny's mum tried to coach her breathing to a steadier rhythm.

Jenny did remember, she had suffered a panic attack very similar to this but not as strong, so she listened to her mother's soothing voice. It was working, her breath was less erratic and at a more comfortable pace.

"Good girl, you're so brave. Sit there I'll get you something sweet to drink, that will help," her mother said as she turned and walked towards the kitchen.

Sitting back down Jenny didn't feel brave she just felt odd. She never had panic attacks at home, so why on earth would she have one now, and so severe? Her eyesight had returned to normal. She watched as her mother approached her with a glass of lemonade. She took it from her mum and smiled her thanks. Her mother sat next to her on the sofa in front of the coffee table with her photographs no longer in neat piles atop.

Jenny took a sip of the cold bubbling liquid and almost gagged. It was revolting, sickly sweet and chemical tasting.

"Eww, mum have you bought a new type of lemonade," Jenny asked briskly putting the glass down on the table.

"No, love that's from the same bottle you had a glass from yesterday," her mother replied, her concern fading slightly.

"Well, it's gone off," Jenny stated.

"Okay, but how are you feeling now," her mum asked whilst rubbing Jenny's back soothingly.

"I'm okay, I think. I feel a little odd, but yeah I think I'm okay now, thanks, mum" Jenny reassured her.

Her mum pulled Jenny into her and gave her a hug. They sat there, Jenny enjoying the comfort of her mother's embrace. They clasped hands, Jenny's skin so pale next to her mother's tanned dark skin. They sat in silence for a moment being held by one another, that's when Jenny noticed her mother was wearing her perfume. It was so pungent and too strong for Jenny. Yet it was her mother who pulled away first, her nose slightly wrinkled in a mirror of Jenny's own.

"Jenny, you should go run a bath, it will help keep you calm," her mum suggested.

"That's okay, mum, I honestly feel much better now." Jenny just wanted to finish sorting the photos so she could persuade her mum to let her out, although the panic attack probably hadn't helped her with this endeavour.

"No, love, you need to have a bath, you're smelling a little ripe. Too much time in those marshes, you're beginning to smell like one." Jenny's mum tried, and failed, to be delicate about the situation.

"Well, I like the smell of the marshes." Jenny shrugged

"Even the stagnant ones?" Jenny's mum raised an eyebrow.

Jenny got up and walked towards the stairs sniffing at her arm. She didn't think she smelt bad, to her she smelt like fresh air and wild spaces, not stagnant pools.

"I do love you, little water weed," she heard her mum's voice soft and sad call after her.

She walked up the stairs to the bathroom, turned on the tap for the bath and added some lavender bubble bath. She went over to the sink and examined her reflection in the mirror. She grinned at herself and as she did, she noticed that her teeth were green again. Confused, she grabbed her toothbrush and paste and started to scrub. She kept brushing her teeth while the room filled with steam from the running bath and the smell of lavender permeated the air. The green was not coming off, if anything it seemed to be getting darker.

Jenny scrubbed harder but the smell of the lavender was becoming really strong, and Jenny gagged even more. Between the disgust at her own green teeth and the sickly-sweet smell of the bubble bath, she felt ill. She gagged again and vomited into the sink. Trailing out of her mouth were what she recognised as water weeds mixed with toothpaste. Her mind raced, she

61

remembered having this taste in her mouth once before, when she was young; mint, earth and sea salt. She coughed and gagged again, more slimy weeds, algae and toothpaste.

The smell of the lavender bubble bath started burning in her nostrils. Jenny was confused. Normally she loved the smell but right now it smelt chemical and toxic. She dropped her toothbrush and clutched onto the sink white-knuckled. She looked down and saw that her fingernails had grown again, into long gnarly points, and were still growing in front of her eyes. Her arms began to crack painfully and lengthen. Horrified, she screamed.

Nauseated and full of panic, Jenny backed out of the bathroom. The lavender aroma followed her, acidic in her throat. She ran down the hallway to the stairs and wretched again; more green algae and slime. She stumbled down the stairs, and saw her mother's horrified face, as she stood up from the sofa. The house smelt so toxic that she couldn't breathe, through the smell of plastic and man-made chemicals. She needed to get outside.

She pushed past her mother who reeked of her caustic perfume, and she reached the front door, turned the latch, and almost fell out gasping for air. She landed on the ground, her chest heaving, her breath ragged. She could see and smell her mother coming after her, she dragged herself backwards on long strange arms.

She felt so sick, and the smell was unbearable. But she could also smell, just beyond her, something better, good in fact, like true fresh air. She followed the scent pushing her screaming mother away and racing towards her beloved marshes. At the first boggy pool, she delved her face deep into the water; it gave her instant relief.

Her mother's arms were pulling her up out of the water. As Jenny's nose and mouth made contact with the air of the up-world, she felt stifled, like someone was clamping her lungs. She could not breathe. Jenny swung her arms back to free herself from her mother's grip.

"You can't go back," her mother cried.

Jenny could not think, she could not breathe. She dragged herself forward to a larger and deeper body of water and flung herself in. She took in deep gulps of water that didn't bring death but freedom. Like the air in her lungs needed to be replaced by water so she could breathe.

It smelt nice down here and she felt at home. An instant peace washed over her. She turned her body in the water and looked up through the murky liquid to the shimmering sun. She could see the silhouette of her mother frantically peering down into the depths.

Did she say I couldn't go back? Have I been here before? - It did feel so familiar.

Questioning her familiarity with this underwater realm broke a spell knotted in her memories. Jenny's mind flooded with images. She, happily floating beneath the water, the woman, her mother? reaching in and pulling her out. She, rushed from freshwater to fresh air, then into a toxic cacophony of aromas. Being wrapped in blankets, the woman pulling water weeds from her hair. Being taken into a bathroom, strange and putrid smells in the air, then dunked into a stinging and poisonous bath filled with strange unnatural bubbles. Being rubbed with towels, her teeth vigorously brushed, the taste of mint, earth and sea salt in her mouth.

Jenny reflected on her entire life at the cottage. How she would become disoriented and sick when she was too far from the marshes? Why had she never enrolled in school? Then there was the fact that Jenny had never known a father, never even thought to ask, like she instinctively knew she didn't have one. Did she not have a mother either? And she instantly knew she did not. But she remembered she did have company down here in the waters, in the time before the cottage. Did she have a family?

As if in answer to her question, she felt arms and hands reaching for her, not from above where the woman was, but from below. They were pulling her down deeper, she looked around and saw green teeth grinning at her. A group of pale-faced, women, water weed for hair, long arms pulling her towards them. She recognised herself in them. She didn't feel scared or threatened by their grasping hands. It was a welcome.

"Jenny," they whispered, "you have come back to us." The weed women spoke in unison. She wanted to go with them. Jenny looked back to where the woman was reaching her hands down into the water. She could smell her stink even down here. It was odd looking at her, she loved this strange human she thought was her mother. But, at this moment, she felt she didn't know her at all. Jenny looked at the fear etched in the woman's face and instinctively reached up to comfort her. Maybe she could come with her, maybe she wouldn't smell so bad once she was down here? She swam up to the surface and grabbed the woman's arms. She pulled her down into the waters, pulling her into a hug. Jenny held on tight, her long arms wrapped around the woman like a vice. She could feel the woman writhing and kicking. Jenny did not understand, why would this woman not want to join her? She had said, she loved her little water weed.

Jenny looked into the woman's face and saw fear and panic, the sounds of her screams caught in bubbles floating to the surface. The woman was not happy to be here, but then her face changed. The bubbles stopped; the frantic movement stilled. The woman now looked calm. Jenny smiled, the woman no longer looked stressed. She had always looked so fraught, well

63

not anymore. Jenny knew she couldn't stay with her, the woman did not belong here, after all, she was not her mother. Jenny looked one last time into the dead eyes of the woman's face, then sunk down into the loving embrace of her green-teethed sisters.

Footnote:
FOLKLORE
This story is a modern retelling of Jenny Green Teeth, an evil water spirit, known to haunt marshland pools in Lancashire. She is known as being pale skinned, with green teeth. She lures children to their deaths beneath the murky waters.

Flood plains

Susan Pope

We are where we are
the house will stay
exactly how I leave it.
We were warned, but until revealed,
the knowledge needed,
nothing is ever heeded.

Guiltily, I
leave the scene seeking
the elusive higher plain.
Birds wheel high in a heavy sky
while dark clouds gather in the
west like crows waiting for carrion.

First drops, an innocent pit-pat, now
icy daggers flay my skin
my coat a black sodden shroud.
Time passes unrecorded. Flood plains grow
the road is a river, I've nowhere to go.
I sink into muddied earth and watch

sheep, cows, horses, in miserable huddles,
heads bowed low, hooves sucked under puddles.
Except for birds, there is no higher ground,
flying high they sing without a sound.
Where is my ark, my solution?
Where is the dove with my olive branch?

A Dying Earth

Angela Johnson

The trees are dead, the wetlands dry.
Sulphur sidles across the sky.
This land is spent, its time is done.
Each seagull scream a fading cry.

The sea is hiding from the sun,
Doomed to die by what man has done.
The earth is bleached, its future bleak.
This planet's old its race is run.

All around this acidic reek,
Choking the plants in every creek.
I feel the earth's deepest malaise,
The world is sick, its soul is weak.

Dawn brings again a smoky haze,
No cause for joy, no cause for praise.
This planet dies and ends its days.
This planet dies and ends its days.

Sting

Ann Smith

One group of scientists are working frantically, trying to clone DNA from all insects and animal life, while another group are trying to grow an artificial food source. Is this because people in power ignored the fact that bees, and sometimes, even pests, were important to the total ecological makeup of the world?

Now all that's left is barren. No sounds of cattle, pigs, pets. No flowers, trees, crops, and no future. The money that was so coveted, is worthless, and the life we took for granted is lost. The planet is dying. It is the ultimate sting.

Don't Weep for Me

Jackie Anderson

"In you go. Step right up to the wall. Now stand still while I search."

Finally, the big policeman gets his hands on me. I think he's been aching to rip at what's left of my clothes, peel open my pockets. There is anger in his blue-stubbled face and callouses on his bear-paw hands. I can understand the search. I always knew there would be mistrust. But I don't understand the anger.

Beside me stands a woman, also in uniform. She writes everything he says to her into a small black book. She is short compared to him, no taller than me, and to me, he is a giant of a man. Her face is pinched with tiredness, and her high cheekbones and sea-green eyes speak of a youthful beauty not quite faded despite the years that have left lines on her brow and at the edges of her lips. I think that perhaps she is not aware that her beauty lingers in the kindness of those eyes.

Her sea-green eyes. I shiver despite the summer heat and have to look away. The memory is too painful.

The big policeman feels down my legs and lifts my bare feet in case I hide something in the soles. He curses. It is one of the few words of his tongue that I can recognise. I almost topple as he bends my legs to show her, and I have to rest the palms of my hands against the wall. I wince, but the cool of the plaster soothes the heat of my sores. She curses too and writes more in her book. When I look at her again her eyes are wet and I have to look down.

Don't shed tears for me, I move my lips but there is no sound. I can no longer speak. There are no more sounds that can escape my throat. No more begging, pleading, crying, weeping, sighing. I am empty. I am silent.

I shed my last tears out at sea. The wind was cold, so cold it tore at my lips, seared my skin. The waves had soaked us and we shivered day and night. She was sick, the youngest of us. She was the last of my sisters. So sick. She burned. They would not give her water. She had been forced to give them everything, yet they gave nothing in return. When I let go of her hands, let her slip away to rest among the waves, there was gratitude in her eyes. I wept until my tears ran dry. Her little face, thin, gaunt, eyes and mouth open, still haunts my dreams. When I dream. I think, like her, my dreams were all swallowed up by the jade jaws of the cruel sea.

"You don't have to be so rough with him," says the woman. Her voice is low and soft, like my mother's.

At the thought of my mother my heart stalls. She might still be in the village, if the rebels haven't shot her, or raped her, or mutilated her. She won't know about Jamila, or Hamed or little Yasmin. She had entrusted them all to me, to the eldest brother. And only I am left.

The woman holds my arm until I steady and the trembling eases. She looks at me and I see her eyelashes are damp.

No, don't weep tears for me. I am here, alive. My skin is flayed by the salt and the wind and the waves. It is blistered by the sun. My hands are infested with sores from the cuts made by the boatmen when they threw dice for my favours, and I fought them off till I could fight no more.

"Torture?" says the policeman. I understand that word. He looks furious. It wasn't my fault. They burnt the soles of my feet before I could escape and take my sisters with me. They were going to be traded for guns, but they managed to drown first. I think of Yasmin slipping gratefully into the water and wish I had drowned too.

"How old?" the policeman is speaking to me but I cannot speak. His English sounds nothing like the words my English teacher taught me at home. But perhaps he is not expecting me to speak.

"About your son's age," says the woman. Her voice cracks and I look at her face.

Don't weep for me, I want to say, I am nothing. I am no one. I am a failed brother, a lost son. I am just the toy of a trafficker, a hunk of meat and bones that no one wants. My face is blank, my soul is dead inside me. I am lower than the lice that gnaw at my sores, less than the crabs that nipped at my toes when I sheltered among the rocks at the edge of the beach where my body, still alive, unwillingly drifted to the shore. It was the sound of an aeroplane lifting into the sky just above my head that woke me from my stupor. It was the dog chasing a ball on the beach that yelped out my presence. It was its owner who spoke into his phone and dragged me into the warmth of the sunshine and tried to help me drink while I squinted at the sun and shrank back at the sight of a wall of stone even those who have travelled hundreds of miles know to be one of the Pillars of Hercules. Perhaps it will be a pillar of safety.

"The doctor's on his way, he may be able to confirm age," says the policeman. His voice is gruff, his hands rough, his movements brusque. "Poor sod," he continues, "if I ever catch the bastards…"

His voice breaks and I look into those sea-green eyes of the woman, the eyes that remind me of little Yasmin, and I try to plead with my silence: don't weep for me. I am nothing.

THE 06.55 FROM COLOMBO

Judith Northwood Boorman

Our grimy train jolts and grinds
Along the dusty sand-blown track.
Clickety clack, clickety clack.
Azure sea, vibrant orange-tinted beach;
Corrugated iron glinting;
Thatches gently rustling.
A crystalline sky gives no warning.

Our train trundles on
Rusty warped track
Clickety clack, clickety clack.
Sandstone stations;
Bougainvillea wilting
In overheated tubs,
The early morning,
Barely cool.

Bodies back to back,
Clickety clack, clickety clack
In the humid carriage
We bump and jostle,
Saris brush suits, brush denim
Scarves swirl their multicolours
From the window's scant breeze.

Inching along the misshapen track,
Clickety clack, clickety clack,
Then in the distance,
Beyond rippling palms.

Beyond the thatch,
The rusty corrugations,
Something strange.

Foaming jaws engulf our track
Clickety clack, clickety whoooooosh
Pounding, pounding waves,
Tossing floppy lurid dolls,
A thousand vibrant flip flops
Surf in the surge,
Then are no more.

Footnote.
During a trip to Sri Lanka, the first couple of nights my husband and I stayed at the rather lovely Mount Lavinia hotel, just outside Colombo. To get to Colombo, we could either take a taxi or be more adventurous and take the train. We took the train. We travelled 3rd class for 15 Sri Lankan Rupees....a bargain...7p! We had to travel on the 'Queen of the Sea Line,' which is the rail line from Mount Lavinia station to Colombo. I had forgotten that Sri Lanka had been so badly affected by the tsunami of 2004. I later learnt that over 225,000 Sri Lankans died in this tragic natural disaster. The tsunami washed away a train of over 1700 passengers. It remains the worst rail disaster in history. Sadly, because of the Christmas holidays and the Buddhist full moon celebrations, there were more passengers crammed onto the train than normal. The tsunami struck between the stations of Paraliya and Hikkaduwa at 06.55. A complete village, Hambantota was wiped out.

Madness

Pauline Odle

Technology brings the world to us each day,

It focuses our minds to what is heard and seen.

We find in disbelief darker days have returned again,

In the shadows waiting there are worse things to come,

History repeats itself, as a mad man reigns again

Like before, a well-oiled plan supports his plans.

How can it be that no lessons have been learned from the past?

As the world prays for answers for the cries for help

People's hopes and dreams have been shattered

As their world has been turned upside down

What price will be paid for victory or defeat?

One thing for certain is that life will never be the same

When the madness is hopefully over

A lot of questions should be asked.

One Day in Her Majesty's Dockyard Chatham

Susan Pope

Based on a true event. Wednesday 15ᵗʰ December 1954

Henry and George pedal as fast as they can with the hundreds of other dockyard maties swarming down Dock Road on their bikes. Once through Pembroke Gate, they leave their cycles in one of the sheds and hurry to the Recorder's hut. If they are late clocking in, they will lose a quarter-hour's pay.

It is still dark this mid-December morning, but spirits are high. One more pay day before Christmas and it should be a good one with the overtime and bonuses. They are working on a refit in number three dry-dock on Her Majesty's Submarine Talent. Henry still thinks *His* Majesty sounds better. That slip of a girl has been Queen for a couple of years now, but it still sounds odd to him.

The chargeman gives them their instructions and they make their way to the stone steps leading down into the dock. The Talent stands upright on wooden chock blocks, her hull buttressed by timber poles. There isn't a sailor in sight. She is swarming with dockyard workers, inside and out. George is a painter and today he must work thirty feet down at the bottom of the dock on the underbelly of the hull. At the stern end, the welders and acetylene cutters are still reinforcing the steel work where rust is being removed. At the bow-end, this work has been completed and the painters have begun their job with gallons and gallons of black submarine paint.

Henry is detailed to a job inside the hull. He is an electrician and a small-built man. He is good at squeezing into tight spaces and pulling new cables and wires through the ship. On cruisers, he is sent up the masts and out on the yardarms. Sometimes he also works on the jib end of the high cranes used in Chatham Dockyard.

The dawn has broken, and Henry reckons it will be a mild, sunny day. That will make a change, for heavy rain of late has had the river Medway running high. Two days ago, nineteen feet had been recorded: that's flood danger level. It has dropped back a couple of feet now and the day is calm. As he makes his way below deck Henry knows he will not see much of it, whatever the weather.

It is half-past three in the afternoon when the workers on HMS Talent hear a terrible crashing sound. The wood-encased steel caisson, which blocked the entrance to the dry dock, has popped out like a cork from a bottle. It is being pushed the three hundred and fifty-feet length of the dry dock by a huge wall of water. George's blood runs cold at the roaring noise as he sees the rising tide of water surging towards him. The river is bursting through the breech, flooding the dock.

The volume, speed and ferocity of the rushing water fill the dry dock so quickly that George is only halfway up the stone steps when he is swamped. He is pushed upwards and hurled over the dock wall then dumped on the roadway like a big fish. Many men do not have time to reach the steps or run to safety. Everyone is shouting and calling for help and the Dockyard alarm bells are ringing everywhere.

The Talent's wooden chock blocks are torn away, and she topples to the starboard. But the rising water fills the dock so quickly that as the flood hits the inner dock wall it rushes back in the opposite direction, picking up the submarine like a toy boat, and dragging it back across the dock. The sub rights itself, but skews, crashing into the dock entrance. Then it is forced out through the gap and into the river Medway, with many men still clinging on to the deck. Some lose their grip and are flung into the water.

Those inside, including Henry, are thrown about like apples in a rolling barrel. The force of the water is so great that the sub is pushed one thousand feet, right across the Medway and comes to rest only because she is caught on a mud bank flooded by the rising tide, at Whitewall Creek opposite the dry docks. By a miracle, she is upright, and boats are quickly able to come alongside to take the shocked and injured workmen off and ferry them to shore. Henry cannot believe his eyes to find they are on the opposite side of the river. He has cuts and bruises but is not even wet, and he thanks his lucky stars he has been saved.

George has joined with others in pulling half-drowned fellow workers out of the flooded dock and other men are being pulled out of the river. Stories are quickly told of frightening scenes and miraculous escapes. George tells of being thrown over the wall and shakes his head. "I was lucky, so lucky." Others murmur in agreement.

A man called Bill tells them: "I was below deck working inside a tank. We were thrown all over the place, but never guessed the dock had been flooded. If she hadn't turned upright, we would have been trapped inside the sub and probably drowned."

By eight o'clock it is known that three men are still missing. A further two are in hospital with serious injuries. Twenty-nine others all have a story to tell of their own amazing escape. It will take a few weeks for the enquiry into the disaster to establish that the huge steel caisson, sixty feet wide and twelve feet across, that should have been filled with water, was empty. It will take a lot longer for the families of the three men killed in the tragedy to come to terms with their loss.

George, Henry, Bill, and the others spend a quiet Christmas with their families, thanking God for their own miraculous deliverance on that fateful day in the service of Her Majesty at Chatham Dockyard.

Footnote:
A fictionalised account of a recorded event written from media extracts.
Story originally published in 'Tales from the Dockyard', University of Kent Press 2010.

Fairy Tales

Michele Barton Macintosh

Fairy tales, something to dream of, something to believe in
Love and laughter, there is always a happy ever after.
Beautiful trees, in summer leaves in luxurious green
In autumn, leaves the colour of browns, rusts, and reds.

Mermaids, swimming in oceans, seas of turquoise, blue and greens,
Whales, dolphins, fish, turtles and seals, swim alongside these beauties.
Coral and shell houses, where they live, sparkling beneath the waves.
These are the things that make us smile, what we wish to dream.

Yet reality is stark, Covid-19 has brought some of us nightmares,
Humans are destroying our planet, with poisons and plastics.
Yet some carry on regardless, still littering the streets, rivers, and seas.
Who can say mermaids don't exist, and if fairies live amongst us?

Humans need to wake up, change their habits, stop being litter bugs,
Stop man-made, use what nature provides, and live alongside it.
In lockdown, no planes, fewer cars, less pollution, trees flourished,
I have never seen such gorgeous, bushes and trees in my lifetime.

Everything is there for a reason, the rain forests, yet we demolish .
The bees to pollinate the flowers and plants; what are we without them?
We have nothing, we will be nothing. Will we be like the dodo?
Let's change all our habits, like we have our consumer habits.

Choice

Nilufar Imam

The Covid-19 Lockdown March 2020 to September 2021

The fearsome ogre struck suddenly, spreading a dark cloud
Of doom and despair all over the world.
The threat brought misery, despondency, with humanity vanquished.
Confronting such a disaster and its ripple effect was devastating.

Undaunted, the brave folks, with resolve, explored ways of recovering.
 Remembering the old saying, "Necessity is the mother of invention".
They paused, focused on their constructive ideas for regeneration,
Emerging triumphant together, with many choices of saving the world.

Footnote:
Impact and regeneration after the Covid-19
Composed for The National Poetry Day on 7th of October 2021

Deadman's Island

Susan Pope

Dead men's bones rise from the silt.
Bone white mouths gape where once laughter spilt.
Arms stretch out from the distant past.
'Take me home, take me home at last.'

Once they were young men: sons and brothers.
Living lives with love and lovers.
Frenchmen ploughing fields or plying trades.
Napoleon called for soldiers and sailors to parade.

A terrible war when the British were afraid.
Scouring their coasts for sight of foreign raids.
Invasion by Frenchies could come any day.
'We mustn't be caught napping, we'll fight them all the way.'

When the French boys landed on British soil
Their muskets ready for fight and spoil.
In an unwinnable war they prayed for a sign,
Found themselves cut down, crossing the British line.

Red coats, Blue coats, toss 'em in the holds.
In prison hulks disease swept through killing many souls.
Those that lived set breaking stones to build the ramparts high.
Brits would not be caught again when the enemy was nigh.

Dead piled into skiffs rowed out to a tufted Isle.
Known as Deadman's Island mid the Medway's muddy mile.
Bodies piled together thrown in pits to rot.
Far from home for them, no sweet French plot.

Now the sea is rising, high tides uncover
Boys denied a farewell kiss from pretty wife or lover.
'Take me home, take me home,' whispers like a feather.
Conservationists try to piece them back together.

How can we atone for the sins of the past?
The world believes it's a different place,
God willing, peace at last.
Will they ever wander in home's sweet embrace?
Leave the hulks and stench behind and the British to their fate.

Footnote.
During the American Civil War and the Napoleonic Wars of the 1700s,
decommissioned ships were used as prison hulks to house prisoners of war with other
convicts, along the banks of the River Medway. The dead were ferried out to
Deadman's Island off Sheppey point and buried in pits. In recent years tides have
exposed some of their remains.

Ashes

Michele Barton Macintosh

As I watch each wave, each ripple
Lap before me, towards my feet,
I raise up a glass of sparkling tipple
I speak words, some ask me to repeat

As I watch, your ashes dissolve beneath the wave,
I feel hands as they reach for me, to help support me
I hear voices that tell me, I'm being extremely brave
Your gone now forever, God never listened to my plea.

Tears spill from my eyes, salty tears, mix with salty sea spray
I turn away from the ocean, listening to the gentle caress,
The gentle caress of waves, moving the pebbles and shells away
Will I forever be this quivering, uncontrollable, heartbroken mess?

War Correspondent

Angela Johnson

And looking for peace where river seeps at last to sea,
and the sky shares its pearl with slow water,
he hears the gulls and curlews call,
and the susurration of tired water,
but there, even there, looking westwards to silence,
in the gulls screaming and the curlew's mourning
still hears the sounds of war.

And in the shimmered gleam of sun on water,
and in opalescent calm,
he hears the children scream.

He's toured the world of blood,
Palliated pain in neat columns,
Now here, as sea mist gathers;
Watching the red in gulls' yellow eyes
He cries in the ripples of the waves.

Young Swimmer

Randa Saab

Let me catch my breath again,
can't hold any more,
That was what the young girl said
as she wrecked on shore.

The engine broke as land appeared,
With no oars on-board
For those who couldn't swim to shore
Azrael drew his sword.

Women, children, elderly
Hearts in death's pan fry
Crying, screaming, praying loud:
For sure we would die.

Bodies falling like dead leaves,
making waves rock high,
Like a stampede in a shack,
There's no place to lie

There was no one to save us,
no moon in the sky,
That was what the young girl said
then began to cry

Death was weaving fishing nets
with the strings of fear
made of hunger and of thirst
ready was the spear,

As we plunged to swim to shore
We heard them calling,
You can push the boat to coast
Save us, bring us in

As one hand we pushed the boat,
Hardly surviving
fighting waves of exhaustion
safely arriving.

Those lost people, strange to me,
in a night so blind
are all that remained for me
of what's left behind.

Footnote: First published in 'On The Boat' Randa Saab2016

The Boy on the Beach

Susan Pope

He pushed his tiny toes into the burning sand and wriggled his little fat feet down to where it was cool and damp. At the water's edge, he could see his father had just pulled his fishing boat onto the shore. The boy laughed and waited for the signal. When the big man had secured the boat he looked up and waved. Little Adou toddled over the hot sand shrieking with laughter. His father lifted him up, swinging him onto his shoulders. The boy screamed bubbling with joy. The man jogged up the beach with the boy held high. It was the best donkey ride in the world and his happiest memory.

Now I'm in the worst place in the world; squashed like a bad melon, faint with hunger, so thirsty my tongue is stuck to the roof of my mouth. I can't move and know I mustn't move. I can hardly breathe as if I lay dying. But I know if I do exactly as I've been told, I'll get back to that happy place with my father. I try not to think about how much I ache and concentrate on more memories; like a video clip I saw once on a phone.

He waved goodbye as his father set off on the boat again. By the shore, he waited for days, but his father didn't return. Adou remembered the soldiers coming to their shack. Father wasn't there, so they took his mother away. After that he was looked after by another woman. She said to call her Auntie. She had six children of her own, so Adou was a nuisance. Food was rationed and being the smallest, he got very little. He wandered along the beach looking for crabs and shellfish. The soldiers told the children to stay off the beach. They put up barbed-wire and signs. He didn't know what the signs meant until the day one of the boys had his legs blown off. After that, he didn't go to the beach.

Worse than being cramped up is the darkness, and not knowing what is happening. Sometimes I am moved and bumped along. Sometimes everything is still. I can hear voices but not what they say. I can smell the sea and feel the rise and fall of the water. I am a piece of luggage folded and creased. The memories return.

Adou had grown taller and skinnier. Every time he asked Auntie about his mother or his father, she made him stand on a stool until he was so dizzy he fell off. If he cried, he was sent outside. 'Snivel in the gutter, gutter child,' said Auntie. He would put his head between his knees, stifling his tears and recall his first happy memory.

One day, Auntie said to him. 'Adou, your father is alive and living in Spain.' He didn't know where that was, but Auntie said, 'That's in Europe. That's where we'd all like to go and leave this Ivory Coast behind us.'

Adou said, 'Can I go there and live with my father?' She laughed at him, but later she said she would find out. He thought that was the kindest thing she'd ever said to him.

Weeks passed, then one day Auntie said, 'Your father wants you to go to him. But you will have to be smuggled in. Once you are there, they won't send you back if you tell them your father lives in Spain.' He was eight years old now. He hadn't seen his father since he was five, but he felt as if he had been dead all that time and now he was alive again; alive and with hope. He also found it hard to believe his cruel Auntie was suddenly being so good to him.

'Thank you, thank you, Auntie,' he said. 'What do I have to do? When can I go?'

'Once you are there,' said Auntie, 'we can apply to join you because we are your family.' He knew this wasn't so but didn't argue. He swallowed the tablets she gave him and slept for a long time.

I am awake now and moving once more. As I lie in my cramped dark prison, the person moving me struggles with the weight. I am scared the hiding place will burst open under the strain of my weight as it moves on the spindly wheels. There is a lot of shouting and I recognise the voice of the girl who has pushed and pulled me on and off the boat. We must be nearly there, very close to the end of the journey.

I hear a dog barking, and my heart is drumming in my ears. Will I ever arrive to see my father? Will I ever learn the secrets of his wonderful life? 'Please let it happen,' I say in my head. 'Please let it happen.'

The dog is still barking and snuffling around; so close I can smell it. My prison is lifted up and then thumped down again; I feel the shock waves. The girl screams and shouts and men are shouting back. She begins to cry. So do I, while the dog still barks.

Hands fumble with the locks on my suitcase prison, forcing them open. My tiny world is suddenly flooded with light, so I close my eyes tight. The stale air I have breathed for days evaporates and my lungs fill with sea air.

Have I arrived at last? Is this Spain? Has my father come to meet me? I open my eyes and see only men in uniform, like the soldiers back home.

Footnote:
Story based on a newspaper account of a child transported illegally in this exact way.
First published in 'Refugees and Peacekeepers, Patrician Press 2017

Nature

Michele Barton MacIntosh

The hands of time are constantly turning,
You can't stop it, wheels are churning
Loves lost, memories fading,
Moments in time never returning,
Why do we constantly have to keep learning?

Take all those opportunities you're given,
Grasp them with both hands, before they're gone.
Your time on earth is precious, it's not very long.
Love, be kind, you may be just one person,
All your actions have consequences, be strong.

Be kind to each other, to animals, to the world.
Generations before us, have left us in this state,
But time will not wait, we can't just sit and hate.
We need to reverse the mistakes we've made,
If we don't, and soon, our planet will fade

Everything on the planet, is there for a reason.
Scientists insist on messing with nature: treason!
The birds and bees, flowers and trees, insects and fleas,
From the ice floes to the Amazon, all have their place
The most destructive animal, sadly, is the human race.

I am the Albatross, What Can I Say?

Kate Young

I soar, I skim the Southern Ocean
scan the surface, dive for squid
my prophecy hung around my neck.

I am reeling, caught in a keening wind
above the billow of black-edged veil,
one last hush of lost soul cull.

The elephant in the water rises
humpbacked, polymers slick on skin
underbelly sleek, awash with waste.

I weep at toxins in tissues of fish
miniscule nurdles, tears of a mermaid
soiling the cheeks of beach and dune.

For ninety days I count the curse
caught in gullet of seabird chick
throat choked in the trash of our age.

A fishing line wraps through broken wings,
scientists rummage through oily flesh
pick the truth from fillet of bone.

I am the albatross, what can I say?

The Journey

Susan Pope

We have many miles to go
journey's end is not in sight.
Hurrying along the shore
board the boat at dread of night.

Babies cry, children whimper
we've no food and little water.
There's no comfort we can offer
pleading eyes of sons and daughters.

We have left the sun behind
where the earth lay scorched by fiends.
Moving north through bitter cold,
rain and mud with bone-chill winds.

Why endure such misery?
Leave old lives behind us.
Living hell, our homes destroyed.
We had no choice, go we must.

We couldn't leave our fear behind
carrying it on our backs.
Weary we walk mile on mile,
now the sea our courage snaps.

Can we find a place to be
together with our loved ones?
Does a haven safe exist?
Will they say: 'not here, move on.'

Will we ever reach our goal?
Like the Nomad tribes of old.
Forty years to wander lost
just as Moses' children told.

Praying not to be turned back.
Queuing at each check-point site.
There are many miles to go
journeys-end our fading light.

Wishing?

Michele Barton Macintosh

I sit on the bench with my cape about my shoulders, the hood covering my head. Red riding hood comes to mind, yet my cape isn't red, my cape is mustard yellow. I stretch my long legs out in front of me, my silk nylons touching my skin, my feet in beautiful lustre boots. I cross my legs and cover them with my cape. Autumn is upon the city. The leaves on the trees are turning from their gorgeous green to gold, yellow and brown. I watch as the sparrows fly, and squirrels jump from tree to tree. The buildings' windows reflect the last of the sun's rays, making the day bright. I look out towards the ocean, watching the fishing boats away from the shore, and the waves gently reach the beach.

Soon, I shall walk to my usual place. I will sit and wait in hiding so she can't see me. I have watched her for three weeks now. Today will be different, today she will see me, now is the time to talk to her. I sit here waiting for the sun to set, as she won't be around until the beach has cleared of people. Eventually, I uncross my legs and stand up, I start to walk towards my usual place, the pier. I smile as I hear my heels upon the concrete pathway. I reach the pier and make my way to the end, out of view, and I sit down.

It's not long before she appears, it never is. I see her, as she flips out onto the buoy. She shakes herself and elongates her smooth neck as she flicks her hair around her head. Eventually, she smooths her wet hair down with her hand. Jet black hair cascades down her back. When it dries, (as it will, the length of time she stays on the buoy), when she moves, and where the pier lights touch her, you can see green flecks, like on a magpie or crow when they move; beautiful iridescent green. Yes, she is beautiful too, her lips tinted pink, black eyebrows, like skinny caterpillars, a pert little nose and her tail, her tail shimmers. It's the colour turquoise; the most beautiful thing I have ever seen.

I wait. I watch her sitting there on the buoy for half an hour. She just stares toward the beach, then she starts to cry. Her tears fall gently down her face and make small splashes into the sea. Quietly, I move, not to scare her. I whisper her name, 'Casandra.' She looks up startled. I carry on talking in a whisper. I don't want her to jump off the buoy and swim away.

'Please don't be frightened, I'm not here to hurt you, I just need to talk to you.' Thankfully she doesn't move, just sits there on the buoy, staring at me, with those big chocolate brown eyes. After what seems like ages she speaks.

'Who are you? How do you know my name? And most of all how come you can see me?' she exclaims.

'I have heard your wishes, your wishes from beneath the sea, the sea where the shells nestle amongst the corals,' I tell her. She lets out a gasp and holds her hand to her breast.

'Oh,' she says, 'Are you here to help me, to help me get legs and walk upon the beach?'

I shake my head slowly, 'No Casandra, I'm not here to help you get legs, but I am definitely here to help, you.' I let out a sigh and try to explain.

'You wish for something, that you have no need to wish for. You wish to walk under the trees, yet you can swim amongst the coral. You wish to run alongside mammals, yet you can swim alongside the fishes, the whales and dolphins.' She is still staring at me, at least she is listening, so I carry on.

'You wish to live with humans, yet you have mermaids and mermen to live with, who are kind and caring. Humans can be evil and so cruel. For 200 years I have been fighting to make humans see where they are going wrong, yet they don't want to see, they are blinkered to what is in front of their noses. The birds, bees, mammals, insects, trees, and nature itself, they walk past it every day whilst they are in their little lives, cocooned in their homes with their TV's, iPads, and mobile phones. They watch stupid things on U-tube, they wish to own the latest cars and gadgets. They want to possess money and they don't care how they get it, if they can buy their gadgets. Even after 200 years they still let the woods burn, the ice glaciers melt, and cut down the tropical forests. Even with Covid-19 they still pollute the world with plastic. Now wildlife is having to deal with their selfishly discarded rubber gloves, disposable masks that have elastic that creatures are caught in and die.'

She blinks. I think things are starting to sink in. 'Casandra, I need your help, because now the seas and rivers are affected. If we don't make them see their selfish ways are killing the planet, our fish and all creatures of the seas and rivers will perish. So, no I'm not here to give you legs, I'm here for you to see what is in front of your eyes for you to cherish, nurture and love.'

I take a deep breath; I try not to cry. 'You asked me three questions, here are your answers. I see you because once I was you, I know your name as I know all your clan, and as to who am I?' I take the hood of my cape with both hands and lower it from my head, my hair cascades down, yes there are greys, but most is still red. She gasps and calls my name.

'Yes,' I say to her. 'I'm Ariel. They didn't tell me I would still live as many years as a mermaid lives but be in human form. I only got to be with Eric for two years before he died, he died fighting a pointless human war. Pointless like all the wars humans fight. Yet I still must live in this form. How I wish to be amongst you all again in the sea with a Mermaid's tail. But I had my wish granted many moons ago. So please, as humans say, be very, very careful what you wish for.'

Another Life

Stella Lambert

Oh, that salt spray on my face,
The ocean wind in my hair.
The forever memories,
I will never erase.

The smell of tar
On the ropes of that old ship.
Bring me back
From somewhere afar.

I was there many moons ago,
It's in my blood.
I'm home under the sails
Of H.M.S. Roebuck.

It was another life,
I could tell you some tales,
Of the times of strife,
Under those
Giant billowing sails.

Part Three
MERMAID SMILES

This section displays work that is light in tone and voice. Written with a smile and a flick of the tail.

Turtle Time
Sulu Sea off Sabah, Malaysia

Angela Johnson

"Turtle time," the ranger calls,
and we follow.
 The sand cracks as day heat seeps.
The moon breaks and bends the sea,
a Sulu siren sings as
warm air like soft fur strokes our faces.

The turtle lies, a monument in sand.
We watch her
In her ecstasy of egg-laying.

Awe is too small a word,
 too big for our gawping,
 as we stare to our beginning.
 Moonlit, torchlight tranced
we hold struggling hatchlings,
smaller than children's hands.
Fingernail strokes in sand follow them to the sea,
One turns back, unconvinced by destiny.
We laugh to hide our sorrow.

Back to beers and books and conversation
We feel losses we cannot speak of.

New World

Susan Pope

Walking on a shingle shore,
Listening to the sea's deep roar,
A twisted shell lay on the beach
Thrown by the tide from Jurassic sleep.

Worn away by wind and water,
The shrunken skull of Neptune's daughter,
As I held its hollow to my ear
Conch sounds sang to me so clear.

An ancient tale of a world new-born,
When earth began, and life was formed.
Primeval roars of giant beasts,
Huge sea monsters in coral reefs.

Trees reaching fathoms high,
Dragons wheeling in a burning sky,
Volcanic eruptions in a boiling sea,
New lands forming for a primitive me.

The Anchorage

Brenda Moss

Pennants fluttering in the breeze,
White-legged men, showing their knees.

Pipes, hats, beards and wellies,
navy jumpers, pompons, smellies.

Shrouds and halyards, pinging and rattling,
jostling for position, friendly bantering.

Steaming mugs of soup and tea,
Thick cheese sandwiches given free.

Screws, hammers, bits and brace,
Varnish, paint, dinghies race.

Long white hulls, skimming by,
Bracing winds, cloudless sky.

Captains' caps, cheery smiles,
Patted backs, ropes for miles.

Sunburnt faces, shouts of glee,
The Anchorage, then off to sea.

Life is Like That –

Pauline Odle

Life is a journey of hopes and dreams,
Like sitting on the beach looking out to sea,
Breathing in the cool fresh air, while your body sighs,
The water trickles across the pebbles close to you.

Your mind goes blank in the sight of the calm moment.
Without warning, your peace is broken as a seagull passes by.
The tide is coming in, and the waves increase in depth.
Clouds turn grey, and quickly rumble your way,

Nature seems angry now, and you don't know why.
Tomorrow finds another day, as the storm has now passed by.
Nothing lasts, life's like that, never knowing what's in store,
A puzzle of events as you go your way and hope your stay to enjoy.

Flying Damsels

Susan Pope

The watercress came from the supermarket
packaged as salad in crinkly cellophane.
I didn't eat it but threw it in the pond.
In no time at all little white roots appeared and
tiny green shoots climbed out of the water
reaching up towards the warm May sky.
In June, clusters of white-star flowers bloomed.

You seemed to know they were there.
Part of the pattern that turns the earth,
rocks it to and fro making the tides ebb and flow.
You came on delicate invisible wings
to see my own little miracle.
Flying marines in blues and reds
mounting shy maidens dressed in green.

In groups, like a troop, or conjoined
in your pairs, you danced your mating ritual,
kissing the white flowering watercress.
Alighting on the water you laid your invisible seed
over and over, just to be sure.
Sure to give re-enactment to this very scene
when May and June come round again.

A Misjudgement

Brenda M Moss

It was a water lily, floating gently in the bright sunlight on the shimmering sea that drew his attention. The tide was going out, taking it away from the beach.

Foolishly, he waded into the cold, turbulent water, oblivious to the fact that his shoes and trousers were getting wet; he was so drawn to the water lily. He knew that the usual place for a water lily was a garden pond, but its beauty and colour drew him ever closer. His thoughts were on his girlfriend; perhaps he should propose?

As he drew nearer to it, he cupped it into his trembling hand, dripping water, but it was still attached to a fibrous root. He pulled it upwards, hoping to release it, but it was too strong. He pulled again, but as he did so a slim-fingered hand, held the other end. He gasped, as the hand locked tightly over his, pulling him down, knocking him off his feet into the water. The thick fibrous stalk wrapped itself around his legs and ankles, anchoring him to the ocean floor. As he struggled to stand up, black eyes and sharp pointed teeth, grinned at him.

'You are mine now,' the Mermaid whispered, through numerous bubbles. "To have and to hold, forever.'

'No,' he replied, struggling up on one knee, lifting himself up out of the water and gasping for breath.

'I am not yours, never. I am promised to another. I love her,' he shouted, as water rushed from his panicking, gaping mouth.

'Mine!' she screeched, pulling him under once more.

'Never,' he finally said, as his head went back under the water. She flipped her tail and turned him, tumbling, over and over in the waves.

'Have you changed your mind?' she leered, through her black sharp teeth, but he couldn't hear her. Then, with a strong thwack of her blue scaly tail, she smacked him back up onto the beach. He lay, gazing up at the blue sky with the water lily kissing his lips.

'Another non-swimmer,' she screeched aloud to the sky. As she lifted her seaweed-covered head up out of the water and flipped her tail once more, she whipped up the icy cold, turbulent waves as she dived back down into the ocean.

The water lily slid from his wet lips, down across the sand and into the ocean, floating gently again, awaiting its next victim. The man coughed violently, turned on his side, releasing the trapped sea water that had filled his lungs, as seagulls gathered and screeched pitifully above.

Grace, a Gift of Love

Nilufar Imam

The clusters of the fragrant blossoms in delicate apricot,
Happy memories of nine years ago, you brought
Presents from special friends, a rose so exquisite,
Celebrating our landmark golden wedding anniversary.

The London Olympics, and the Queen's Diamond Jubilee
Held in 2012, the significant year of history
Leeds castle in Kent, standing on islands in the lakes of river Len
The romantic venue, 500 years ago visited by King Henry V111.

The formal dinner was in his banqueting hall
With the portrait of the Tudor King on the wall,
The staterooms for us and accommodation for friends to stay overnight
In the tranquil surroundings of the castle and moat was utter delight.

The sunlit breakfast room with past royal connections,
The table spread of the delicious local produce inspired awe,
Culminated in our fairy tale dream come true,
Here is hoping that 2022 will be our diamond Jubilee

The River

Ann Smith

Cascading clearly from the hill,
It falls to rest against its will,
Winding round the muddy banks,
It shows no anger, speaks no thanks,
On and on not daring to stop,
Never again will it reach the top,
Spraying dew and crashing on side,
All in an effort to reach the tide.
The seas in view at last it's here,
But wait, in front there is a weir,
Rerouted, deflected, it tries to fight
But soon the sea is out of sight.
Running swiftly through a town,
Running on, and down and down
To a lake that's long, deep, and wide
Sliding past the great divide.
The scenery here is very green,
The sky is blue, the best it's been,
No more running to the sea,
This is its final destiny.

The Beach

Susan Pope

Ted felt a thrill as the train stopped with a jerk. He looked up at the station sign: MARGATE. A smile warmed his face. By the time he reached the seafront, it was midday, and he looked out to the horizon. White clouds dotted the sky and white horses topped the waves, racing each other to the beach. Ted gripped the rail and carefully negotiated the steps down to the sands, catching the aroma of dried seaweed stranded at the high-water mark. The air was cold with winter bite, but the sun shone with fresh spring promise.

Ted breathed heavily trying to find his bearings. He'd met Janice in Margate. He'd come down on the back of his brother Alf's Harley. He remembered how hot they were in their black leathers in August. Janice minced along the prom with some other girls. She wore a red mini skirt and a skimpy top. They were giggling and trying to catch the eye of a group of mods; suave chaps in Italian-style suits, leaning on their Lambrettas and Vespas. He remembered running his comb through his black hair, pushing it into an Elvis quiff. He'd stepped right in front of the Mods and stopped Janice in her tracks. They'd smiled at each other; one of those instant clicks. Ted marvelled he could recall every detail of that day, yet he couldn't remember yesterday.

After he'd bought Janice a coffee at the beach café, they had walked along the beach, away from the crowds of noisy Mods and Rockers filling the promenade and spilling onto Margate beach, distancing himself from anything that might spoil his mood. He'd felt shy, embarrassed almost, by this lovely girl, by the fact she had been happy to walk away from her friends, with him.

Janice told him she was a trainee nurse and he'd said he was an apprentice electrician. Ordinary lives, ordinary people. He'd put his arm round her shoulder, and she'd leaned into him as if she belonged there. By the time they'd walked to the far end of the bay and rounded the headland into the next cove, Ted felt they had been together forever.

He stopped and looked back. He couldn't see Margate beach anymore. It had disappeared like yesterday.

That first walk had become a wonderful life together. How long had it been? Someone said it was fifty years. Ted stopped walking and watched the tide turn and begin to creep back up the beach. He remembered that first day like yesterday, that first walk with Janice, better than all his other yesterdays. That was why he'd come back. They'd told him he'd lost Janice, but how could he lose her? Now he'd found her again on Margate beach.

The sun had disappeared behind the clouds, grey and heavy. But Ted felt warm inside. He was holding Janice's hand as they walked down to meet the incoming tide. They stopped and faced each other. Ted thought his heart would burst with the love rising in his chest. The wind blew her hair, and he smoothed it away from her face. They kissed; a perfect first kiss of new love and an eternity of love to come, as the water lapped around their feet.

Ghost Ship

Ann Smith

I feel so honoured to have been shown
A tea clipper ghost ship coming home,
With its masts and sails of pearly white
Its brass work polished, and gleaming bright.

Though no shipmates seen working on deck,
It's clear from the image, the ship's not wrecked,
As it floats lazily upon the blue-grey sea
Before the dawn sun has risen free.

So silent when it passed my way,
No creak nor bell nor sailor's bray,
Dipping and listing as waves break beach,
Perfect, a vision, just out of reach.

Then just as it falters and breaks on rock,
Five o'clock chimed on the old hallway clock,
Daybreak arrived and the sun shone through,
Then translucent ghost ship vanished from view.

The Octopus

Brenda M Moss

I am an octopus,
did you know?
I have eight arms!
It should be so.

One each for my children,
One for my father
One for my mother
My husband and lover.

All pull them together
which way shall I go?
Perhaps you will pull them off,
I just do not know.

You are all pulling so hard,
Let me pause for a while,
Just leave me alone,
To rest in my cave.

Symphony for Grey Marsh Dawn

Susan Pope
Inspired by Oare Marshes at Swale.

First movement is adagio. Grey leaks
across the sombre sky. Largo from the east
meets moist mist lifting from the marshes. Soon,
gull wings stretch rising into the grey gloom.

As waders and marsh birds leave safe night roosts,
tempo allegro, busy beaks forage for food.
East winds stir seed heads and shake grasses grey,
there sounds a percussion, soft timpani.

Grey fades away, drummed by day. Big skies start
the metronome, synchronised with feathered hearts.
Music flows cantabile, glowing with new light.
Chorus voices trilling in high delight.

Wild horses in warm coats graze tough grasses.
Stamping hooves sink in boggy marshes.
Ancient breeds thrive in this wet cold place,
solid as oboe, cello or bass.

Ermine-clad solo artiste; lone white egret
oversees chorus birds who grovel at his feet.
He will not sing today, his presence fable.
Suffice he enraptures, lord above the rabble.

Flowers pink and ochre with green grasses sway.
Water reflects blue sky and sun's midday.
When twilight returns, ancient vespers sound
a deathly slow march. Keen eyes see vagabonds

and ghostly smugglers, meeting murderous ends.
As barn owls screech, white wraiths fly the ebony
sky. At first light, the symphony spawns
a silence, a prelude to reprise; grey marsh dawns.

A Devastating Tale of Disobedience

Angela Johnson

"Don't you go near that pond, girl,
dangerous."
Dangerous: a sound that grown-ups make,
when you're four, the world's new,
you're bored
Adults gone to their secret world of busy,
puppies sleeping, not playing,
and the cats are chasing mice.
One finger in the pond won't hurt.
Green stuff slimes its surface,
Bit smelly.
Smelly doesn't hurt when you're four,
and the admonishing world has gone away
to round up cows and pigs.
Lean a little closer.
That naughty imp called curious,
Pulls me down to subterranean slimes of times past,
The spinning world of almost death,
That sudden saviour: grandad, old corduroy and smells of shit.
"I told you, girl,"
and there I am
returned, the incredible little hulk,
all snot and slime and tears,
back to the world of sun and scolds.
"Don't you go near that pond, girl."

Flatford Mill

Susan Pope

Inspired by the landscape painting by John Constable

I am so very proud to have been allowed to ride our mare. Jenny is a shire; she stands at twenty hands yet gentle as thistledown. She pulls the barge with the tow. Up and down the path we go, taking whatever the master says. Coal from the open caste, gravel from the river. Iron from the smelt and wool from the hill sheep. All pass through Flatford Mill on the way to market.

I could ride Jenny all day, her back broad as Pa's armchair. I walk her up the towpath, but she needs no guidance. Her hooves plod with soft hammer blows. Her harness rings like church bells calling all to prayer. I pray days will always be like this: me, Jenny, and the lazy river.

Spring

Debra Frayne

How softly comes the Spring.
A dream that wakes from Winter's slumbers.
The gentle light of morning sun
Warms and stirs quietly to life.

Green shoots, curling sprout.
Faithful leaves unfurl from empty limbs.
Busy bees buzz among the blooms
A symphony of spring in motion.

Songbirds rouse the dawn with their chorus,
Trilling, warbling, joyfully calling.
There is so much to do. Awake! Awake!
A new day comes! Awake! Awake!

Seeds planting, snails wandering
The new and green springs forth.
Scents and aromas glide the breeze
Welcome again for Spring is here.

Winter Morning

Jackie Anderson

Morning air so cold
it slices through your skin
and peels back the last of night-time sleep
from eyes that sting in thin
winter light so bright
it glints rose gold
from silver leaves.
Each step a snap,
a crack, a sharp shot,
each breath a shard of icy mint
that lingers on your tongue,
then leaves the scent
of musk, of earth,
of naked trees,
of frozen dew
…of death.

What's in the Bathroom?

Judith Northwood Boorman

I go into the bathroom,
I really have to laugh
I gasp, I shriek. A big surprise…
There's a crocodile in the bath!

The ducks aren't very happy.
There's a look in old croc's eye
He flashes teeth and smacks his lips
The ducks all start to cry

"Help us! James, come quickly!
That croc looks full of glee
Save us, please, from his sharp teeth
Or he'll have us all for tea! "

The Lake

Susan Pope

Nahuati pushed his boat from the shoreline and leapt aboard. He punted the little craft out towards the reed beds. Nahuati was nineteen and very proud of his boat, built by him in the traditional way by tying bundles of reeds together into a long waterproof platform, then forming raised sides and a high prow, which he'd fashioned in the head of a condor.

As he punted from the shore, he lifted his head. The lake stretched out before him, as big as an ocean. The water looked as blue as the tail feathers of the giant macaw. He breathed the cool air, so clear, he could see for a hundred miles across the width of the lake to the snow-capped mountains on the far horizon. The sky above reflected the same brilliant blue as the water of the lake. Above this glorious scene shone the life-giving sun, sent by the sun god Inti. Nahuati imagined it was just as it must have been on the first day when Viracocha the god of creation had brought forth the sun, the moon, and the first humans from the waters of Lake Titicaca. Nothing had changed.

Another boat hove into view and Nahuati waited until it drew alongside him. The punter was a girl. Her name was Hotia. She came from the Island of the Moon. Nahuati lived on The Island of the Sun. Both islands were at the centre of the lake and were sacred to the Legend of Viracocha.

In the stories of old, if a man and a woman made love when the sun and the moon were in total eclipse, their union would be blessed by the gods with children and good fortune. Nahuati loved Hotia, and he imagined he was the sun, and she was the moon. Nahuati wanted good fortune and perhaps children, but most of all he wanted Hotia.

Footnote:
Nahuati means four waters. Hotia means - dance.
(South American traditional names.)

Nature

Ann Smith

Have you ever stopped to think, what nature really means?
Of all the things that live on earth and swim beneath the seas,
The waking in the morning and the smelling of the dew,
The little bird up on the wing as he flies out of view,
The trees in their glory, the flowers in the park,
The insects and their enemies that come out after dark,
When sunset fast approaches, the moon appears so blue,
That's what nature really means, not just me and you.

And in the honeysuckle's shade, a dragonfly will eat,
While rabbits hop and skip about on their enormous feet,
The bees, bats and butterflies, the slow worm in his quest,
The wading birds in clear lagoons, the squirrel's stolen nest,
And in the wood a fallen tree, a welcome insect ark,
The rotting wood gives life to moss and fungi in its bark,
Wildflower meadows softly sway, as sticklebacks swim free,
That's what nature really means not just you and me.

The mountains and the valleys, the foothills just beyond,
The sheep that graze the hillside, the cattle by the pond,
The funny little farmhouse, that's painted red and white,
The collie you hear barking, though he's just out of sight,
As chlorophyll drains from the leaves the countryside will weep,
Then winter comes, the scene turns white, and nature falls asleep,
But soon the spring will warm the earth and life will start anew,
That's what nature really means not just me and you.

The Confluence

Nilufar Imam

The alluring sight of the glossy leaves climbing the frame
 Of our seagrass blue gazebo set against the azure sky,
Nourished by the recent deluge of heavenly water,
Displaying the scented white flowers of star jasmine
 Beckoned a closer look at the adjoining Madonna lilies,
In full glory, pervading the air with their sweet fragrance.
So intertwined were they, with no edge or boundary betwixt,
Water from above failed to eradicate the confluence of perfumes.

One

Michele Barton Macintosh

Have you ever looked at a single petal on a flower?
Or a leaf attached to the strongest tree?
Have you ever looked at a single grain of sand?
Or just one pebble being washed ashore by the sea?

Each one is needed to make the bigger picture,
Each one joined to another, makes something beautiful,
Each one has a purpose, each one has a story to tell,
Each one, somehow, is just like me and you

The Day We Buried the Fish

Lin Tidy

The Lido, on the line that separates Margate from Cliftonville, is an acre of sea-filled square, cut off from the open water by a two feet wide wall on which we can walk 200 feet into the sea without getting our toes wet. Walking to the end, a 90-degree left turn takes us another 200 feet, parallel with the horizon, and then another brings us back to the beach, sandy on the right when facing out to sea, and rocky and slimy on the left.

We'd fished for shrimp around the wall. Isla and Solomon had learned the rule; only one rule for my grandchildren in a world of rules:

'If we can't eat it, we put it back to continue living.'

Solomon had broken this rule once and watched, without emotion, as tiny crabs scuttled around in a plastic bottle searching for home until they tired and died. So, the rule was spoken again, this time in a firmer voice, locking eyes and speaking of, 'the rights of crabs and all creatures.'

We searched those slippery rocks, which held on to the sea in their cracks and dips and folded chains of weed. To return to the same place and never find it again is as wonderful as travelling the world, each rock pool exotic and new with the leaving of the tide.

The day we buried the fish had been such a day; a day of carrying and digging and building and imagining where those ships, now anchored, and dancing, had travelled and fought their passage through green and foam, glass and storm.

The fish was half hidden in the sand. A good foot long, its fins were open, as though death had caught it in mid-swim. Solomon took a sharp breath and grew frantic in the find.

'Let's bury it! he shouted. 'Let's give it a funeral.'

His usually off-hand sister, older by two years…or twenty, caught the shout and joined in. Even the dogs seemed to catch the mood, digging holes and running around, their tails damp and salty, breath cloudy and warm.

It was the perfect day for a funeral.

Footnote:
Originally published in: The Day We Buried The Fish, 2017

Part Four   **MERMAID WRITING**

This section contains stories, poetry, and memoir pieces with a diversity of themes.

In Liz's Shoes

Judith Northwood Boorman
A Concrete poem (formatted in the shape of the theme.)

                    I always longed
                      to be in Liz's shoes.
     The Imelda Marcos of Chatham; wardrobe
     bulging with well-shod shelves, for every
                      occasion
                    in dazzling
                 hue: a shoe.
               Glitzy
             salsa slingbacks.
          Soft suede mules. Dolly
        shoes, pink, blues, spotted, bowed,
      killer heeled,
      narrow-
     toed.

                      But now I despair
                       and don't care
                       to be in Liz's
                       shoes. Her
                       wardrobe
                        is bare,
                        except for one pair
                      of sensible flat lace-ups
                      for support and balance,
                    When really what she
                    actually needs is a
                    pair of magic
                    crystal slippers.

.

Background to 'In Liz's Shoes'

I wrote this shortly after my dear friend (and surrogate sister) Liz, gave me two black bin liners filled with her shoes.

She was diagnosed with motor neurone disease in August 2017. By February 2018, she could no longer wear her shoes with heels.

Over the subsequent years, her mobility and speech deteriorated.

Despite that, she remained independent, determined, and inspirational. She went to Westminster, speaking on behalf of those with MND to the All-Party Parliamentary Group. She continued to work as Kent Community Foundation's Office Manager until she could no longer speak.

She was, for most of her life, involved with the charity sector, working in both Scotland and England. She moved home 17 times in her life, following job opportunities. Liz always helped others.

The inevitable happened in February 2021 MND won the battle and claimed Liz as another victim.

Please help the Motor Neurone Disease Association to support the research to find that magical crystal slipper – a cure for this awful condition.

Footnote 2: See page 4 for details of Medway Mermaids' charitable donation from book sales to MNDA.

Pretty in Purple

Jackie Anderson

Just my hat and I'll be ready to go. It's purple felt and matches my purple wool coat. They cost me weeks of my pension, but they're worth it. And they both match my purple hair. I chuckle just thinking about it. My hairdresser thought I wanted a purple rinse. But I wanted electric purple, and had to go back with Lucy, my great granddaughter_ the one who speaks little, and studies a lot, has her eyebrows pierced and wears her hair in shocking blue spikes – to convince her. Lucy thinks I'm batty and she's probably right. She's a little bit crazy herself, but that off-the-wall nature will serve her well in this topsy-turvy world.

I have a penchant for purple, always have had. I would have worn purple on our wedding day. but Ted was as strait-laced as my veil and I gave in and wore white.

My younger sister Carole's special weakness is black leather. At 78 she's a bit of a young blood compared to me, and she doesn't think twice before pulling on her leather thigh-highs over her jeans, zipping up her studded jacket and perching pillion on the back of her son's Harley. I admit I envy her a bit, but with my right hip the way it is these days I've no intention of slinging my leg over a motorbike and hanging on to some muscle-bound biker, appealing though the thought is.

I grin at my reflection in the mirror; a little twirl, a sassy glance over a shoulder, a pout and a dab of pink gloss and perfect. Now my walking cane and I'm ready for Ted's big day.

I open my front door just as my neighbour roars off on his Kawasaki. It's green and he wears a matching kit with a yellow stripe across the full-face helmet. With a beer gut draped over the engine he is like a ridiculous locust buzzing about for food. Decades on from when I used to ride with the Angels, I still only turn my head for the deep throated growl of a Triumph.

Ted had cars, three of them at one point. The Fiat was for ferrying the kids to and from school. The Stag was for show and the Volvo was for towing the caravan on our holidays. Once we were married and the kids born, I never sat on a motorbike again.

But that never worried me. Ted would tease, especially when Carole would talk about the festivals she'd been to, or the rides. But then Carole married Liam who built motorbikes. I married Ted the teacher, who was warm and loving and fun, even if it was fun in a quieter way and without the chemicals. I've enjoyed every minute of every year I've had with him.

It's a little bit of a walk to where I'm going, and I have to take small paces. My route takes me through the dull landscape of brick terraced houses, so I pop in my earphones to pass the time. I have to turn the volume right up these days, but no matter. I downloaded some of my favourite tracks last night with Lucy's help. I pick some Fleetwood Mac; easy-going and catchy.

The sky is bleak, a dash of meagre light between the rows of dark red roof tiles that line the path to Ted's special do. I have received dozens of offers of lifts but I turned them all down. I like to walk. Ted and I used to go for long walks in the country, picnic on our backs and a blanket for sitting on grass. We used to take our kids, and then their kids and even their kids – although more leisurely by then.

The music doesn't seem to fit the mood. I stop, take off my pink fluffy gloves and fiddle with the phone. That's better. The intro chords rasp and music from Pulp fills my ears. Common People. Exactly as we were, Ted and I. Ordinary, common people. That picks up my adrenalin a bit.

At the end of the road, a bleeping interrupts the music. I press a switch and push the microphone closer to my mouth. I love technology. I would say I'm a silver surfer but I'm most definitely purple today.

"Gran, are you on your way?" It's Lucy.

"Of course I am."

"I thought you might be put off by the cold. Or that you'd forgotten."

"How could I possibly forget!"

"Don't be late. Call if you want a pick up."

"I wouldn't miss today for the world, love."

I always went everywhere with Ted. He filled my life. We lived together, laughed together, even cried together sometimes. Wild horses wouldn't keep me away today, even if he does disapprove of purple hair. I know his way of thinking. Just like he can read my mind. "You wear your feelings on your face, Kitty," he's always said.

My emotions, if not totally dried up, are a little stale today. I wonder if they become worn with age, just like fingerprints do. I need to crank it up a little. Today is also about fun. If there is one over-riding feature of our lives, it has been fun. I try ZZ Top and that makes me grin. ACDC

127

and their dirty deeds done dirt cheap has me chuckling, which I think the postman I toddle past finds disconcerting.

At the roundabout, I have to concentrate. There are pedestrian footpaths and toucan crossings and flashing lights. A flutter of panic crosses my stomach and I hesitate at the edge of the road, a dual carriageway heading towards the motorway. I have a fleeting desire to hail a taxi and get there early. Ted is very insistent on punctuality. Natural for a teacher. He was a drama teacher and a fine actor. He was never late for anything. I was never early, not even for giving birth. I was never late for his performances, though, and I shan't be today.

I feel hot. I yank my gloves off and one falls to the ground. I curse loudly.

"Here you are, my love," says the postman. He picks up my glove. He seems flushed; blond hair streaked with grey and face like a beetroot.

"I'm about to cross over," he says, talking loudly, which is just as well because Metallica is blasting some whiskey in the jar into my head, "would you like to take my arm?"

I would if you looked like young George Clooney, I think, but then this hero is to hand and Clooney definitely isn't.

"Thank you, dear." I grip his offered forearm more tightly than he expects and he winces.

"What are you listening to?" he asks once we are safely on the other side.

"At the moment, Thin Lizzy," I tell him, "but I'm thinking of resting a moment and setting up a Marilyn Manson versus Slipknot medley as I walk down the hill."

I can't help grinning. His gawp asks for it. Except I shan't listen to that. That's my angry music and I don't feel angry today, just like I don't feel sad or sentimental.

I take my hat off and shake my hair loose. Whoever says old ladies can't have long hair? I let it tumble about my head as it always has done. Ted, who was so precise, such a rule-follower, a perfectionist, a conventional man loved me: me, unruly, impractical, unpredictable me. The attraction of opposites.

Instead, I pick Take That. The Circus. Ted liked it, just as he took a childlike delight in the circus with its clowns and trapeze artists and magic. It was how he first entered the world of make-believe that led him to the theatre where he could be whoever he wanted to be. Otherwise, he was happy to be just plain Ted. My husband, Ted. Now dead, Ted.

At the gate of the graveyard, I pause. In the distance, between the trees, I see a large gathering of people and recognise our family and circle of friends. Carole and her husband are there, their motorbike leaning against a tree. Lucy and her friends are there too. They all loved Ted. He was teaching drama classes right up to the day before he went.

I think those words: "he went" like he's nipped to the shops. But he's gone for good.

I take my earphones off and tuck them into my pocket. My back aches a bit now but I walk forward. Ted will be waiting for me like he has had to so many times before. And I won't be making him wait too long. I can feel myself reaching for him and I won't fight it. I just intend to have fun while I still can. He approves of that.

I pretend not to notice the raised eyebrows. Ted would have laughed at them and enjoyed me being me. He always thought I looked pretty in purple.

The Bond

Susan Pope

September 1944

Now is the dog-end of a war that still has miles to tramp before it can be over.

A new-born baby gasps and takes its first full breath. It yells at the world with angry words it has yet to learn. Mother hums a lullaby, a song reused from siblings. Their father has never witnessed any of the births. Always abroad, at sea, at war. She pulls a basket onto the bed. Third-hand nappies, muslins, cot sheets. In the bottom, she finds a pair of pink crocheted booties. Never worn. This is the first girl, but she will be the last babe.

The day is warm, the window ajar. A butterfly lands on the sill, turning round, sunning itself. It takes off again. She wishes she could do the same, leaving the burden of her life for others to endure. The baby at her breast gurgles and she looks down. Her nipples are engorged, the colour of red wine.

'Oh, happy child. If you only knew the task I have placed on your tiny shoulders. He is coming home. His war is over and so is his affair. His madness he called it. Perhaps it is you, little one, bringing him home. I pray you will be the bond to bring us back together.'

December 1966

The ingredients had been bought weeks before, but time had not allowed the making. One week before Christmas you declared, 'Today, I will make the puddings and write the cards if it's the last thing I do.' How I wish you had never said those words, not those words.

You mixed the sugar and fats with the eggs, all creamed together in the red plastic washing-up bowl, adding the flour, the fruits, peel and nuts. Six silver thru'pennies, used year on year, were twisted in greaseproof and hidden in the mix. You called and said, 'Come on, stir and wish.' Me, with my red painted nails, too old for such childish whims, played dumb. But now, how I wish I could rewind that day and change the outcome.

130

You wrote the cards, and no one helped; not me, head full of selfish, romantic dreams. You walked to the corner alone and pushed them into the red pillar box. The red washing-up bowl was covered with a damp tea cloth. You said, 'Tomorrow I will fill the basins and give first boil.

Your tomorrow never came. Instead, Angels came and took you away in the night. I finished your task on Christmas Eve, adding my tears to the mix. We carried on, grief too raw to share, like lost blind mice. Without your love, everything that had held us together began to crumble. Soon we would fall apart and scatter.

December 1973

I find your knitting patterns. I sew your stitches. I am back at the place where I was born. Your labour pangs are now mine; I feel your presence. The fierce and clinging love of my new-born child leaves no room for unrequited grief, it is banished by the suck and pull of her need to survive.

Outside the day is dark and gloomy. Storm clouds vanish in the magic mix of my astonishment at her arrival. Her bright blue eyes leave rainbow hues in the winter sky. These first precious hours reveal more than a genetic link. I look into eyes so wise and see another. I walk with you once more gathering wildflowers. We pick blackberries and laugh together. Oh, how good it is to hear your laughter. She holds your fingerprint. I see your footprints, and we walk in the shadow of your love.

A past life is reborn, but it is a fleeting miracle. Soon, the echoes will fade. The footprints washed away with the incoming tide. She will grow into her own self and write her own history.

The Happiness Thief

Catriona Murfitt

The happiness thief is a prickly fiend,
He comes disguised as a fail or loss,
But whether you want him there or not,
He seriously doesn't give a toss

He doesn't care about your poor feelings.
He just wants to bring a dark black cloud
When you want peace and quiet, my love,
He likes to make your world seem too loud,

But this foul beast has a major weakness
And that weakness is actually you,
As he thrives on care and attention
So, here's a little trick you can do:

Fill your life with wonderful distractions
Friends, family, hobbies and your work,
Shine a bright light of activity
So there's no more darkness for him to lurk.

He shudders with every hug you receive,
He shrivels at the pure sound of your laugh,
And when you say I truly love myself
It's like a sword that cuts him in half.

Please be brave, my sweet, for this demon
Is not as strong or scary as you think.
Live life in wonder, keep your hope alive,
Smile fully and watch that beastie shrink.

Agent Allison – City Slice - *An extract from a novel in progress.*

Jayne Curtis

Cruising down St. Clément's Boulevard, the red Mustang, aka 'The Rental', sliced through the crisp air that was blowing in on a light breeze across the bay. Water slopped against the man-made cobbled beach, whilst the city's lights danced, stretching far out across Lake Michigan's dark waters. The Rental parked up. Too early to join the other muscle. The lights rested on the Ford's hood, adding energy to energy as the music throbbed deep and low over the clearing roadways. Five minutes to midnight. Five minutes to race time.

The square began to fill with wheels. Their cool crews added to the energy buzz. Official wheels paid to keep a slow response time.

"Hi, Sky? How's it rollin', babe?"

Sky's head almost hit the low skirt of the rear axle. Spanner in hand, she pulled herself out from under her car. Why did Cam's deep, sexy voice always have this effect on her? Oh yeah, she knew why; she so did.

"Cool, dude. Real smooth," she replied as she wiped an imaginary mark off her shiny pink Nissan Skyline.

Cam nodded, keeping his eyes on her. "She's looking good, just like her owner."

"Awe, don't you tease me, Cam. So, how's your ride? You got a grip on those huge four cylinders yet? That super turbo-charged monster is pretty powerful, even for you."

His face broke into a slow smile, the way he often did, his way, that way. "Don't you worry about me, Sky babe, I'm going all out. I'll watch you all still cruising from my rear-view mirror."

She didn't doubt it. You could hear the F-Bomb Camaro even with the engine switched off. It oozed power from every cell. "I reckons, I can still give you a run for the prize money."

"Sorry, babe, but I'll be back here collecting that wad of greenbacks way before you bring your skirt home."

She smiled a slow smile, the way she often did, her way, that way. She would certainly try. Her new cylinder layout meant she had two more horses that he didn't know about.

"Let's hang out after the race. I'll treat you to a drink with my winnings." He knew she wouldn't say no.

"You two should get a room and be done with it!"

"Rino!" Sky squealed. "It's so good to see you." She hugged him. He didn't resist.

"Hi, man. Looks like you made it just in time!" Cam slapped his friend on the back.

"Good to see you, Cam, Sky. It was a bit hit n' miss. I'm parked up next to the Dodge. It's so pimped out with all that green spray and twinkling lights, it's making my wheels look respectable."

"Don't be fooled by appearances, man. The aerodynamic gives it the extra enhancement it needs," Cam looked over at the Dodge. "So, that's your Gran Torino? Nice." He nodded his approval.

"Yeah, but I'm only a playboy next to you guys. I'll give it a shot, but I'm just here for the atmosphere."

"Don't run yourself down, man, you got what it takes." Cam slapped him on the back again.

"Looks like a good turnout tonight. It'll be one hot race, that's for sure," Sky said as she scanned the vehicles. "You have a gift too you know, Rino."

"Thanks, but against this lot, be real, Sky."

She was about to answer but the growl of an arriving engine made them look up.

"Bitch!" Cam's shoulders seemed to square up just that little bit more.

"Might as well go home." Rino's voice fell flat.

"Why?" Sky asked.

"Mustang Sally. That's why," Cam growled.

Rino laughed. "That car can sustain a drift like no other. And I've seen it change colour with ma own baby blues."

"Don't be silly, Rino," Sky said. "You exaggerate so much!"

"I'm telling yer, it glows."

Sky shook her head, smiling wryly. "You'll see her off, won't you Cam?" ignoring Rino and his silly comments.

"Hah! She creamed him last time, didn't she, Cam?"

Cam's eyes narrowed. "She did. Any other car I'll see off, but Sally, she's a whole different badass ride."

"I'd like to meet her. Get some tips."

Cam and Rino looked at Sky. "Good luck with that!" they said in unison.

"She don't ever stop for the prize money, neither." Rino added.

"Wonder why? I mean, what's the point?"

Cam watched the Mustang approach. "Cause she can, to prove a point. Got to admire that, even if she is a bitch."

"Wonder who she really is?" Sky's brain was ticking over faster than her car.

"Yep. Might as well go down the beach for a swim," Rino sulked. "Fancy a dip, Sky? The night's perfect."

Sky laughed. "No, I think, what I fancy is trying her on for size."

"After me, babe, after me," Cam's voice had a new edge to it, one she hadn't heard before.

The Mustang stopped in front of them. The driver's door swung open. It seemed like time didn't exist. A hush descended, silencing the loudest of engines. Mustang Sally stepped out of the car. She walked up to Cam. "I owe you an apology." She held out her hand, keeping eye contact. A few long seconds later, he took it.

"Yes, you do."

She pulled him to her and kissed him. The kiss lasted longer than the handshake as Cam cupped her face in his hands.

"Apology accepted," he whispered.

Nice. She thought.

She smiled a slow smile, the way she often did, her way, that way. "Drink, later?" She knew he wouldn't say no.

Sky and Rino stood there watching, speechless.

The Rental took its place in the line-up. As the flag rose in the air, she mimicked Captain Gregson's chastising voice, "Not exactly official use of resources, Agent Allison!"

So is.

The flag dropped. She hit the gas.

The Law Woman - *a novel proposal*

Jayne Curtis

FBI Agent Gina Allison discovers the journals of her great-great-great-grandmother, Amber Rose Allison, who was one of the first law women in America. Dating from 1860, the haunting entries are sketchy, some written in blank verse. They tell of Amber Rose's harrowing ordeal following the death of her husband and son at the hands of outlaws, who had also kidnapped her younger son, Frank Junior, aged 5.

Journal entry – After the funeral – October 1860
Widowed at twenty-nine
My Sherriff husband ambushed
Our eldest son caught in the crossfire
Our youngest snatched.

I could have taken to the bottle, some wished I had,
I did not.
What I did was pick up my husband's badge, pin it on, and declare myself Sheriff.
There was no objection. Nobody wanted that job on the lawless frontier of Arizona.

The bounty on the Brolin brothers grows
They laugh
They terrorise
They continue to kill.

I have vowed to take that bounty
to find my son.
My sweet innocent child
I fear I am your only hope.

Journal entry – October 1862). (in the desert
Two years hence,
My Life. My Son.
Dust drains my lips
I feel no more
Beaten
So tired, searching, I must…

We rest now
The Black Quill and I, I try at least
You'd love him
You could ride bareback he wouldn't mind

The fire dwindles
But not my burning soul
My soul knows you are out there
Somewhere, I must…

I long to hear your laugh
My son
Stay safe
Under these stars above the desert lands

I pray
you didn't see
them perish
your father, your brother.

Out of this dust I will rise
Out of this hallowed ground, I will find you
I pledge this
Keep my spirit with you

When I find you
Until I find you
My veins run black with agony
Will the end never come? I must…
find you.

Who Needs Maps? *Written as a 100-word challenge*

Pauline Odle

I don't get lost; I take scenic routes.

On one occasion, after a brilliant day out with my brother, the return journey was different. There were delays on the roads ahead of us, so I took a diversion via the green lanes of the countryside.

My brother had the map. Unfortunately, I forgot he was dyslexic and did not know his left from his right. I was awaiting further directions when the answer came.

"Please yourself. The dog has put his paw through the map and eaten the missing bit!"

No idea where we were, but we got home eventually.

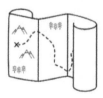

Just One More Time

Brenda M Moss

From swerving fast cars, to comfy armchairs,
Sipping tea, instead of Champagne.
The crossword replaces theatres,
Life will never be the same again.

Gone, are the roses and kisses,
Van Gogh and walks by the Seine.
His every step is now painful,
How I want my man back again.

Throughout the night I hear him,
His breathing, loud and sparse.
Old age seems longer, than his youth,
I long for these days to pass.

He lays so still beside me,
Those hands I knew so well.
I now hold them, as his mother.
If only I could tell.

I am loyal to his memory
That lover, bronzed and strong.
How I treasure those passionate embraces,
When nights were hot, and long.

His lips and eyes still ask me,
I answer back with mine.
Oh come back, my darling lover,
Just, one more time.

Broadstairs by Boz

Debra Frayne

I confess that when I travel, I never arrive at a place, but I immediately want to go away from it. Not so Broadstairs. Sunshine and sea air work wonders on the spirit of man. Or, at the very least, this man, in this most humble of modes. One feels one's lungs expand in delight and the tang of salt on the breeze lends one a sense of soaring freedom. As the gulls fly like swirling children rejoicing loudly at their flight, so do I in much-subdued form.

As always the bright visage of chalk cliffs erase any sense of melancholy and bring one firmly back to oneself. A promenade along the bay heralds treasures of a modest sort to delight the senses. There are fine places to find sustenance and, I confess, some amusement at the characters found in the streets below the grand house in which we stay.

I have just returned from my morning constitutional after which we stopped at the Inn for our luncheon. While at table, we beheld the most dreadful scene of licentiousness. The poor woman, clearly in her cups, had gotten up on the table and started to sing about being part of the furniture! One wonders at the quality of this particular native having had no such experience on previous occasions. I was not able to offer my assistance, as moments later, the woman was taken away by some base-looking fellow followed closely at heel by his soppy nanny dog. He was clearly embarrassed, poor soul. Perhaps this is a regular occurrence for them. Hmm, might be that my muse is leading me to further tales to be told. There is always something of a story to be made in every experience.

It was the best of times; it was the worst of times. My constitution has taken a turn for the worse and I suffered a malaise inside the house, in the shadows unable to go further. I can only blame some unsuspecting whelk sampled on the promenade of the seafront earlier today. This mono-chromed half-life is mirrored outside perfectly by an ethereal fog that has blown in on the evening tide. The mist has made uncertain ghosts of houses and trees and the world has all but disappeared in a shimmering blanket of swirling grey. In the moments when I can bear to stand, I catch glimpses of a smoky world with darker shadows moving about within. I fervently hope that this insidious and violent phase shall pass quickly and tomorrow shall again return to brighter times.

Thankfully all has returned to normal. We stopped for refreshment at Miss Mary's house. The woman is quite obsessed with the donkeys that occasionally pass by her door and will insist that they do not. Sending out the maid to hinder them one way or another and sometimes even herself. One wonders if she is trying to set up some sort of private toll. For all intents and purposes, a fine solid woman, made ridiculous by donkeys. Or, one could say, she has made an ass of herself.

As I consider that our time away is coming to an end, this time spent in reflection and restitution turns my mind around. Where will we be years from now? Will the troubles that beset us now be ended? Will we have righted ourselves and be working towards a better world? I hope ceaselessly that it will be so. Perhaps not in my own lifetime but surely in my grandchildren's time. Or, maybe, 'tis all but a bright dream envisioned in this idyllic, hopeful place making my thoughts sanguine and reassured where they have previously been waxing both bleak and dour. Nevertheless, I return to the world, refreshed and full of vigour, looking to do my part in bringing this dream to fruition.

Footnote.
Written in celebration of Charles Dickens' connection to Kent.

The Cornfield   *Inspired by John Constable's landscape painting*

Susan Pope

The sky is clear and blue and everything shines with reflected brilliance from the sun at the top of his arc. Tom has been out since daybreak, scaling the hills and shepherding his little flock back towards the farm.

Hot work, sticky weather. One more turn of the path and the stream comes into view. It laps the banks in dappled shade under oak and elm. He runs, leaving the dusty path and throws himself on the nearest bank, dunking his head under the surface. He gulps mouthfuls of glorious liquid quenching his thirst. With eyes open he sees minnows dart and freshwater shrimps somersault through waving water weeds. He is so hot he wants to dive in and swim with the creatures; become a water-babe.

His dog barks and he lifts his head remembering his task is not yet complete. The dog waits on the path, wagging his tail, guarding the sheep.

'Good dog, Ben,' says Tom, 'walk on.' The dog resumes his role, nudging the sheep along the path, patient as a goose-girl.

Further on they stop near the entrance to the cornfield, where the grass is sweet. The sheep will graze here for a while. Tom sits on a bank, gazing over the golden corn. It's ready for cutting and Tom will help bring the harvest home. He lifts the cloth from the basket and unwraps his pasty. He feels a little thrill remembering Maisie's words.

'Here's your lunch Tommy. I made it special for you.' The pasty is packed with tatties, carrots, onions, and shreds of mutton. Ben comes close and wags his tail in expectation. Tom laughs and tosses a pastry crust into the hedgerow. Ben dives for it and is surprised as dozens of multi-coloured butterflies take to the air in a cloud, startled from where they had been dreaming in the sun.

At the bottom of the basket Tom's fingers find the cool earthenware bottle. Will it be water with perhaps a drip of ale? He pulls out the stopper and takes a swig. He smiles from ear to ear, Maisie's home-made ginger beer, sweeter than wine. He puts the stopper back, saving some for later. There's more work ahead and the day is still hot, with hazy skies full of the end of summer. They resume their journey: the sheep, the dog, and the shepherd boy, whistling the tune of a song he'd heard Maisie sing, as she worked in the kitchen back home on the farm.

The Dream House

Judith Northwood Boorman

She had never intended to move. The little Medway village where she currently resided had been the best place she had ever lived.

Well, apart from Fugen, in the Ziller Valley, Austria. Now that place had been spectacularly beautiful but was never a permanent home.

Memories flooded back of their small wooden chalet, overshadowed by the looming mountains.

In winter, a sparkling pristine white and in summer a lush vibrant green. She loved watching the beautiful iconic Austrian cows, chewing the cud, with an occasional swish of their tails or quizzically studying her with their doleful brown eyes. The sound of their tinkling bells echoed throughout the valley.

Yet it was merely a ten-month idyll. An extended holiday after three years at Kent University. It was a fantastic routine. They worked in the morning, from February until April, then off skiing every afternoon.

The sense of freedom when you pushed off at the top of the black run, hurtling down the snowy slopes, the icy wind and biting ice crystals bringing a red glow to the cheeks. The adrenalin rush knowing you were seconds from potential disaster. Just a slip, a cross of the skis could send you cannoning down, arse over tit, to potential oblivion. She loved that sensation. She became an adrenalin junkie over those three months.

The summer was tame in comparison. Until, of course, her sister Melissa and brother-in-law, Alex, came to visit. It was going to be the last big trip in their gleaming, open-topped, Triumph Stag. She was having a baby in September.

Melissa said she would never have kids. Her dogs were her babies. Now here they were, her sister and brother-in-law, a blooming Melissa, struggling to get her already expanding belly out of the low sprung sporty Triumph Stag. That was so long ago.

Danielle, her niece, now thirty years old.

Suzy had moved to her lovely Kent village thirty years' ago too. However, something had changed. Since retiring, her stunningly beautiful village had become boring. Nothing happened.

She had exhausted the delights of the numerous glorious walks. Now only one dreary weekly coffee morning in the cramped Portacabin. She had

143

gradually dried up, running out of conversation.

She could not drive either. She was confined to bus or train. Her husband had died of a massive heart attack. A huge shock. He had seemed so fit. Her niece's children, however, had provided a distraction during the holidays, childminding Jemima and Jack.

Ironically, she would have loved to have kids, but it just didn't happen. Instead, she had a very successful career, travelling the world extensively, both on business and for pleasure with her wonderful husband David.

She found it a bit frustrating though, on the child-minding front, as there was only one rather uninviting playground within walking distance. She could not even take them to the library every day, as the library was only open half the week. A sad waste of one of the village's precious resources.

Then one day her niece, Danielle, had a day off and they went to the seaside. Normally they would head for Broadstairs, which was one of their favourite Kent coast towns. Yet it was always very busy on the beach. You had to fight for your square of sand for the kids to build their sandcastles. In the quaint town, the French tourists would jostle for the space on the narrow pavement.

Instead, they headed to Westgate-on-Sea.

'Oh that's funny' she told Danielle on the car journey. 'I've just remembered your nan and grandad looked at properties there.'

They parked, with ease, alongside the sloping green sward of lush green lawn.

Suzy surveyed West Bay. The colourful and artistic well-maintained beach huts, the sandy beach stretching far into the distance on the receding tide, and the neat café. It was undergoing building work. A smart upper terrace and chic restaurant, enclosed in glass, gleaming with an aura of newness.

'I can't believe I've never been here before.' Suzy mused as she sat overlooking West Bay sands. She wondered about property prices. Similar to Whitstable perhaps? Prices there had rocketed since the high-speed train. Also, the popularity of the 'Whitstable Pearl' novels had added 'book tourists'.

When Suzy finally returned home, she was salty, tired and happy. The sea air's restorative zone tang had revived her sagging spirts.

She researched the area. She didn't realise Margate was steeped in history. The recently redeveloped Royal Sea Bathing Hospital, had been a sanctuary for sick people with scrofula. The condition of the lungs sounded most unpleasant.

144

Suzy, by contrast, felt excited, alive and with a new sense of purpose and vigour; definitely the best in a long time. Certainly, since David died.
Perhaps she should investigate the property prices in Westgate?
She had quite a shock.
The first property to pop up on Zoopla was 'The Dream House.'
Just from the first photo, she was smitten.
It was beautiful.
Exactly the sort of house both David and Mum would have loved, if she had been able to afford it.
She read the sales blurb:

'Steeped in history this superb detached Georgian maritime residence constructed in 1791 was the first property to be built in Westgate. By the 1860s it had been developed into the 'go-to' resort for wealthy Londoners looking for a place by the coast and nicknamed 'Mayfair by the Sea'. The house is only a 30-second walk from the promenade and beach.

Westgate is also a very friendly community with a village-like atmosphere. It has some charming and individual retail outlets including a unique parade of individual canopied shops and cafes as well as an excellent and inexpensive three-screen cinema." *

The romance of this lovely place, steeped in such history tugged at her heart. She felt spirals of excitement unravelling the knot of anxiety she had been carrying, since coming home and entering her lonely house.
Her heart missed a beat when she saw the price.
At 09.00 exactly, she was on the phone to the estate agents. Her hands were shaking with trepidation. On answering, she blurted to the agent:
'I've fallen in love with The Dream House. When can I view it?'

Footnote
House description courtesy of Fine & Country Estate Agents, Canterbury.
This short story won First Prize at the Westgate-on-Sea Literary Festival 2019.

Easter Memory   *Written as a 100-word challenge*

Pauline Odle

Easter, when my children were young, was time away to relax. The location for our trips was Mockbeggar in the New Forest. A delightful cottage with immaculately laid lawns for our daily games of croquet.

The preparations began immediately with the painting of the eggs and making biscuits. Sunday, we awoke and went to a dinky church in the heart of the forest. After the service chocolate eggs could be seen and eaten. The family came together for a large roast dinner.

Then we all went out the back garden gate for a long walk passing ponies in the forest.

Burning Stubble

Brenda M Moss

From Allington Lock, on the upper reaches of the River Medway, in Kent (where it meets the tidal Medway) we knew that we had approximately nine more locks to pass through, before reaching our destination of Tonbridge.

After Allington, we had passed through several of the locks on our way upriver and soon came to a very quiet area, taking us under a low wooden bridge. We wondered, as we arrived, whether the boat would go underneath that bridge, but it did without a hitch.

As we motored on, we could all smell burning, and up ahead were a group of boys crouching down on the riverbank. On the right-hand side of the river, was an official Scout camp site, in full force. There were several adult Leaders, and young Scouts milling around. A flagpole stood in the centre of the campsite. Green, patrol ridge tents had been erected. To one side, was a larger white marquee type, mess tent. The boys seemed to be busy with their various tasks. Near the water's edge, as an adult leader held one end, several boys were attempting to board canoes and there was a lot of laughing and teasing going on. On the left-hand side of the river, however, three teenagers were attempting to light a small fire, alongside one of the wooden supports of the small pedestrian bridge, that we were about to pass under.

We shouted across to them. 'What are you doing? You will set the bridge alight, you fools! Stop it.' But the response was a mouthful of abuse, two-fingered salutes and we could see that they were basically showing off to the Scouts and trying to copy what was going on, in the official campsite. Contemplating stopping the boat, we suddenly noticed that one of the Scouters, alerted by our shouts, was soon making his way from the campsite along the bank, towards the bridge and the unruly teenagers. Excitedly, they had started jumping around, having lit their dangerous fire. Our boat motored on, and we could see that the Scouter, by his determined walk, was heading in their direction, carrying a bucket, to no doubt sort them out and extinguish the fire. As we glanced back, the teenagers tried to catch up with us, running alongside on the towpath, possibly intending to jump aboard, but fortunately, the river veered away from them and meandered into a type of pond area where there was a choice of two bridges under which we could travel. We motored under the right-hand bridge, leaving the left-hand bridge for boats coming in the opposite direction. Vessels travel past each other on water, on the opposite side to that travelled on the roads in Great Britain. We all, I suspect, mentally, waved a relieved goodbye to the troublemakers.

As we continued, we suddenly found ourselves enveloped, by thick, white, choking smoke. Not just a few wisps, but vast amounts, which swirled all around us and for a moment, we were unable to see the direction we were headed for. Then, we could see higher up the bank, that a field was alight. The fire was spreading across an area of cut corn stubble, the flames leaping skywards, as we passed. The smoke was making our eyes water and for a while, it was quite a worrying situation, as we did not know where the river was taking us. Then with huge relief, just as suddenly, we left it all behind and emerged into another quieter section of the river.

Ahead, stood tall reeds, and saplings on the riverbanks and at the water's edge, reflecting in the water. A swoop of swifts darted above our heads and all around the boat. It was peaceful, we were in an area away from people, the villages, and the farmer's fields. We all sat daydreaming, enjoying the moment, as we emerged twenty minutes later into another aspect of the river. This time, the water was churning, and up ahead, we could see a huge lock looming up high in front of us, with brick walls on either side, daring us to enter its gaping mouth.

'This looks a big one,' Den said, as we eased ourselves up from our various seated positions on the deck, and aft cabin seats. With hearts thumping and great trepidation, the lock key was located, and with widening eyes at the prospect of what was in store, we all took in a deep breath as we gazed at the huge, high lock gates. We had arrived at Hampstead Lock, menacingly tall, bricked walls, formed a deep cul-de-sac. Water trickled and leaked ever so slightly, through huge lock gates ahead of us, as onlookers, on both banks of the river, smiled with raised eyebrows and murmuring voices.

'This should be worth watching,' someone commented within earshot. Eager anticipation was written all over their faces.

Den steered the boat, holding onto the tiller, into the lock space, towards the huge wooden gates, keeping her steady. I managed to throw a line from the front of the boat, to an eager, interested male who was standing above our heads then, on the riverbank. He secured it with great professionalism to an iron ring set in the ground. I made my way up the high, rust coloured, bent runged, iron ladder, hand over hand, not daring to look down. Den threw another line, from the rear of the boat upwards again, the same man caught it, and he secured the second line in place, leaving a lot of slack in the rope. Our next job was the lock gate behind the boat. Already there was help at hand, as helpful ramblers and our two daughters made their way (after also climbing the ladder) and running along the riverbank. Suddenly several people all lent a hand by leaning against the wooden arm of the lock and half sitting, half walking backwards, they pushed the huge lock gate closed on our side of the riverbank. We had to run ahead to the second closed lock gate in order to walk across the top of it, to the other bank and then run back along the bank to the first lock arm, where again, helpful onlookers all helped with turning the key, turning the screws and pushing the lock gate back into position. Ahead, the forward lock gate was gradually opened, again using the lock key, to wind up the giant screws, as the mechanism gradually allowed the water to rush into the cul de sac, which was holding our boat, from below. All the while, our boat was tossed around by the force of the water entering the lock. Gradually, our boat lifted up to the level of the river ahead, until the lock gates could be fully opened for us.

As we moved carefully away, thanking our many helpers, there, moored up and untying their ropes, was another boat ahead of us. As we left the lock, with friendly waves, they inched forward into the space we had just vacated and the whole process was repeated by everyone again in reverse. Our little family gazed back triumphantly. That was one lock that we were all glad to leave behind us. Surely, there would not be another as tall and as frightening as Hampstead Lock. Would there?

Love Story

Michele Barton Macintosh

She looks at her reflection in the mirror, noticing the wrinkles around her eyes and mouth. Smearing her red lipstick across her weathered lips, she puckers up at the reflection. She tucks her hair behind her ears, picking up a diamond earring, gently pushing it through the stretched hole in her earlobe.

Her brush has seen better days. As she pulls it through her silver hair, another diamanté falls silently to the floor. She gazes deep into her eyes, where once the pools were deep blue, now they seem a dull grey. Yet the sparkle is still there. Or is it a tear? No, definitely a sparkle. She gives a heavy sigh. The breath seeps out through her mouth like a tornado. Oops, too heavy, as a noise escapes from her rear. She places the brush back on the dresser, pushing herself from the chair. She takes her walking stick and hobbles to the bedroom door, viscose skirt tucked in her knickers, Nora Batty hold-ups, for all to see.

She holds on to the handrail with her other hand. As she manoeuvres down the hallway to the living room, she peeps around the corner, to see her husband snoring in his favourite chair. His shirt collar turned up, tie lopsided, hair fluffed to one side. He gets so tired these days. (He has waited 2 hours for her, to put on her makeup.). She calls to him gently, as she doesn't want to give him a heart attack. He helps her into her coat, discreetly tidying her skirt, shaking his head with a smile.

They take thirty minutes to get in their car; walking stick gets stuck in the door; handbag spills out on the ground. They eventually arrive at the venue, a hall decked out with silver and gold balloons. Cheers and shouts as they enter. Adults and children align the hall. These are their children, their Grandchildren and Great Grandchildren, celebrating their Golden wedding anniversary, for this is their love story. Without them, the others wouldn't be here.

Find Your Blue Sky

Catriona Murfitt

Today is like blue sky,
Full of hope of a sunny day
Where anything seems possible
And troubles seem far away.

Each new moment a blessing,
A chance to take a better route
To find a piece of happiness
A far worthier pursuit.

My hope is never failing,
No matter the darkness around.
It won't give up, it will not hide
It knows that like can be found.

This world is ever changing.
The good or bad, this too shall pass,
So embrace those special moments,
As nothing ever does last.

Your life is how you see it,
A curse, a blessing, or a gift,
So if you are stuck in the dumps,
Give your gaze a little shift.

Search out to where your life is,
Follow it, keep faith and laugh,
Find your art, your craft, your love,
And if that fails change your path.

Happiness can be fleeting,
But so are the woes and strife,
You need the rain for the rainbow,
So make peace with that in your life.

There are no rules, set patterns,
No specific road, or true way,
Be open to change direction
To find your next blue sky day.

The Social Evening

Brenda M Moss

In the late sixties, on my way to work, I often purchased a copy of 'Woman', or 'Women's Own', magazines. This helped pass the time during the tedious journey to work, from Gillingham High Street, to Strood, on a crawling double-decker bus. I then had a half-hour walk to my office as a Shorthand typist. (I worked in the offices of one of the factories at the very top of Knight Road.) I enjoyed looking through the magazines, as there was always some new hairstyle or fashion, that I was interested in copying, like many other young teenagers, I suspect. Often, they had special offers which interested me, and I would send off excitedly for the item being shown that week. I recall sending off for a copper kettle once, only to find that it was just a thin copper covering, over the kettle. I still have it. I gradually learned over the months, just what the word naivety meant!

However, one purchase that I was particularly thrilled to receive from the postman, was an orange (all the rage) ready-to-sew jacket and skirt, (then known as a costume or suit.) I made a lot of my clothes. Skirts, blouses, curtains, and children's clothes were all within my capabilities. So, the ordered suit, I knew would be easy for me to tack and machine, possibly in a weekend, and I enjoyed making it. The colour was as depicted on the model in the magazine, and I had fortunately ordered the correct size. I laid out the pieces and enthusiastically placed them together, tacked them into place, and machined them together, on my late mum's inherited, old treadle sewing machine.

Within a few days, I had finished the suit. It was perfect. After pressing, it fitted me like a glove, and the very next week, I bought myself a white blouse to go with it. The front of the blouse had layers of lace from the neckline down to past the hips. It was sleeveless and went well with the suit. I added white stiletto heels, a white handbag, and white gloves (we all wore matching gloves with our shoes and handbags in those times.) With my bouffant hairstyle, I very nearly matched the model in the magazine. All I needed was the occasion, and the very next week, it came, in the shape of a social evening, with my boyfriend's yacht club.

The night of the social evening, he smiled at me admiringly as I settled into my seat in his Morris Minor car, and off we set. It was to be held at a local church hall. Thoughts of music, dancing, and perhaps a Babycham, beckoned. I adjusted my skirt and smoothed down my lace ruffles as we entered the church hall. I glanced left and right. It seemed to be full of what appeared to me, to be, really old men. I felt myself take a sharp intake of breath, as I glanced at the rows of chairs facing a white sheet pinned up to the wall in front of a stage. The room was divided into two parts. In its centre, was a small aisle, at the top of which, stood a machine set on a tripod. That evening, it was my first experience of a projector showing a film.

We took our seats near the back, on the left-hand side at the end. A man stood up in front of the sheet and thanked the members for coming. He hoped we would all enjoy the two films being shown that evening. There would be a raffle for the club's funds. He hoped that we would all purchase tickets before the film commenced. The raffle would be drawn during the interval along with refreshments.

The first film (a documentary) was mackerel fishing (or was it herring?) in the North Sea. I rolled my eyes. The second would be a surprise! A few members clapped. I sat down onto a very hard, upright, wooden chair, and the lights were all switched off, after the curtains had been drawn. A loud voice asked everyone to put out their pipes, and cigarettes, in case of a fire, and we all waited for the film to start. After some light cursing from the projectionist, we all listened to the cultured commentator, as he explained about how the mackerel (or herring) were caught. Not what I had anticipated for my social evening at all.

Suddenly the lights came on. To my left, a folding shutter was thrown up, with great force, and a loud female voice bellowed out.

'Tea in ten minutes. I'll bring round the food first, then you can queue for your teas.'

Some men stood, pipes were lit, and several of them made their way to the rear of the hall to the outside. Suddenly, the elderly, matronly type woman, elbowed her way through the kitchen door, holding a large white enamel bowl. She stood at the end of the first row and instructed the men to, 'Take one and pass it on.' They all complied. Her voice was enough to make us all do so. As she came to me, seated on the end, I glanced down into the white enamel bowl, where I could see a collection of large, brown, fat, and greasily shining, cooked sausages (I'd had my tea.)

'Take one then' she insisted, as I hesitated, then, gingerly, and cautiously, lifted a greasy sausage from the bowl, and she shoved a white paper napkin onto my lap. I seemed to be struggling with the weight of the bowl in my right hand and little left finger and was conscious of my new orange jersey suit and white lacy blouse.

'Pass it on,' she insisted, and with my right hand, and my left hand's little finger, weakening and supporting the bowl, I managed to right-elbow my boyfriend, who was talking to another member of the cruising club, on his right. He suddenly noticed my predicament and grabbed the bowl, took his sausage, and passed the enamel white bowl on.

Licking fingers, a queue formed in front of the kitchen, and sturdy mugs were filled with strongly brewed tea, from a large two handled tea pot. Milk was splashed from a glass milk bottle, heaps of sugar added from a cut glass sugar bowl and stirred into their mugs. Several stuck the used spoon back into the sugar bowl. The person at the end of the queue probably enjoyed a large tea-stained lump of sugar in his own mug of tea.

I glanced down at my skirt, as I retraced my steps. All was well fortunately. My skirt and blouse were not grease or tea stained at all, luckily!

'We now have a surprise for you all' announced the Club Social Secretary. The lights went off, the shutter was slammed down and amidst loud crashing of mugs from behind the screen, a short film commenced. We watched, as a member showed his narrow boat holiday, on the Norfolk Broads. He stood at the back, alongside the projector, explaining who was who, and where was where. Loud cheers went up, every time he appeared on the screen.

As the evening ended, groups of men stood outside the hall chatting. I returned several smiles, as I realised, I was probably a bit over dressed for the cruising club's film evening at the local church hall and very much in the minority as far as the fairer sex was concerned. There was after all, only me, and the very tetchy Mrs P present and not one Babycham or dance had materialised all evening. I did wonder as we drove home whether Mrs P had used the white enamel bowl to do the washing up. Removing the left-over sausages first, of course!

Garden

Angela Johnson

In a garden you might expect epiphany,
A metaphysical firecracker whizz across the sky.
What do we have? A woman on a bench,
A yellow cat grown cowardly in old age.
Alert for enemies of youth.
Too old now for agitations of bristling fur.
The sun is washing out the bleach of winter,
 A shy visitor smiling apology.
The woman looks at the fence,
Worn by wind and rain and time.
She smiles at the first mint
in a plastic bucket cracked by winter ice,
and the cheap necklace of spray as
Sparrows wash.

Expecting awakening after winter,
The woman, always, as the cat,
A sleeping thing,
Smiles at the sun.
Looks at bright heather in tubs.,
remembers
Welsh moors in August.
One day collecting blueberries in plastic boxes,
She and her brother,
Mouths and hands stained purple,
Skylarks calling, and the sun insistent,
a buzzard mewing, and the girl laughing.

The Twig

Debra Frayne

The dusty, cloaked figure strides along the narrow forest path between the new spring green brush. His steps are sure and steady speaking of the many miles he has travelled. Heavy lidded, brown eyes look at the sky through the canopy above. Dusk is approaching and he must soon make camp for the night or risk getting lost, or worse, injured in the dark. An ancient fir tree appears round the bend, its dense skirt full and round providing ample shelter for this late spring evening. A traveller's pine, a welcome sight. Pushing through the brush he finds himself beneath the branches next to the rough, red trunk and makes his meal after coaxing a small fire to life. More for the light than for the warmth offered. The sounds of the forest settle but the traveller has been away from home for some time and is feeling the need for company. There is probably no one around for miles. He takes a knife from his side and slices at a twig he has found lying on the ground and he mutters a secret incantation, breathing life into the small form.

At first it seems as if nothing is happening, but ever so slowly, two eyes open in the lichen covered wood. Bright hazel eyes open for the first time to the world. And then blink, and blink again. A tiny mouth opens and a timid tongue, the colour of green wood licks at the brown lips. Arms stretch and the twig bends itself and kicks its legs getting a feel for its limbs.

The enchanter smiles at the stick.

"Well met, friend," he says. The hazel eyes spin slightly and then focus on the man's face, widening slightly as he sees clearly for the first time. He stares intently for a few moments and then he too smiles. The mouth works for a moment as if trying to speak and the enchanter holds up a hand.

"Take your time, it will come to you, all the words you need are there for you. Take a breath and the right ones will appear."

The little stick man sits up in the flickering light and breathes the forest air, rich with the scent of pine.

"I fell from the tree and was dying. Now I have life though I am no longer part of the tree. How is this so?"

"I have been travelling a long time and know much of magic. I have not spoken to anyone for days and would have some conversation this evening. Please, may we talk?"

The stick pauses, deep in thought then replies. "I am not sure what I could offer a great magician such as you. I am a simple stick and have never travelled. What could I talk about that would be of interest?"

The enchanter smiles again. "Let me worry about that."

The next few hours are spent deep in conversation. The enchanter wants to know all about life as the tree. About the passing of the seasons, how the sap ebbs and rises with the cycles of the moon. How the trees converse with each other in their own language and how each tree is in itself a multitude of voices all singing together.

"It would be wonderful indeed to live in such harmony. I wish we men could manage such concord." The enchanter looks sad. "I am travelling to see this land's King. He has summoned me. There is trouble brewing with the country to the east. It is ever the same." He sighs. "I thank you, friend, for your companionship this evening. You have given me much to think on but now I must rest as I still have many miles to go before I reach my destination."

The stick man murmurs his accord but does not understand tiredness having only just been brought to life. As the enchanter lies down to sleep, the stick man's eyes are drawn upwards to the place where he used to be attached to the tree. His conversation with the enchanter has made him sad and longing for his place with the tree, the only home he had known.

He only has to look a moment, and then his decision made, he starts his climb. The climb is very difficult for one as small as he. The branches are so very far apart down near the base. He manages to find handholds in the rough scaly bark of the trunk and slowly progresses upwards.

It is lucky he does not feel tiredness. It takes most of the night to climb the great tree to the place near the top from where he had fallen days ago. He finds it and touches the broken stem longingly but there is no going back. The sap has already stopped flowing and the inner flesh is starting to go brown where it has sealed itself. He sits down on a nearby branch and looks out with his new eyes.

The sky is lightening now, and he watches as the golden light grows above the horizon. His viewpoint is high above the rest of the forest and gives him an unobscured view all the way to the mountains.

He feels as though he can see everything from here and he finds he can recognise things he has no knowledge of. He can see a river winding its way from the mountains off to the north-west. The forest stretches for miles in each direction and the sky domes over it all.

As the fiery golden orb of the sun inches higher and higher, its warm rays finally touch the stick man where he sits, a tear in his hazel eye. The dawn is indeed beautiful. As the dawn light touches him so the enchantment ends, and his last breath sighs out of him as he falls to the ground once more. No magic lasts forever.

The Bull and the Garden Gnome

Brenda M Moss

Houseproud women, who cared about their upholstered suites or armchairs in the fifties, draped antimacassars over the backs and sometimes the arms for protection, to prevent soiling. Antimacassars were made with various decorative patterning. Mainly white, they were often embroidered or had cut-out filigree edging. Whatever the housewife preferred, or could afford they obviously bought.

Macassar was a hair oil used by some of the male population, to keep their hair in place. There were no gels or hairspray in those times. The working-class equivalent was Brylcreem (favoured by my dad and uncles) I watched with curiosity, as they brushed and combed their very long, top hair, which they grew and combed back from their foreheads to the lower back part of the skull. The lower neck hair and sides were razor-cut very short, (favoured by servicemen everywhere). This style was adapted by those males leaving the forces, having completed their National Service.

On Sunday mornings, Nunk was to be found in the kitchen of the prefab peeling the potatoes and carrots, he had grown in the back garden. He would chop up carrots, swede and cabbage, shuck peas, and place all these vegetables into their appropriately sized saucepans, above the unlit gas jets All was then prepared, ready for cooking later, by my aunt. The small joint of meat was placed into the oven. He always prepared the vegetables, every Sunday morning, for the whole of his married life. Then, chores done, he changed into his Sunday best suit, applied a liberal amount of Brylcreem to his hair, kissed my aunt goodbye, stated, 'I am going to see a man about a dog,' and left.

'See you this afternoon,' she added, as he closed the back door. He was meeting my dad and uncle Charlie at the pub, for their Sunday get-together and family catch-up. This Sunday ritual, remained the same for years, as did my aunts, and I suspect many other housewives, of working-class males.

In wintertime, we amused ourselves with jigsaw puzzles or board games as my aunt sat knitting, occasionally looking at the clock and listening to the radio. Sunday was a day of rest. Some went off to church. Eventually, my aunt stood up, went into the kitchen and using a box of matches, lit the gas rings underneath the saucepans, which were ready and waiting.

'I don't suppose they will be back before the pubs close,' she would state, as we two looked at the clock, stomachs rumbling, salivating at the enticing meaty aromas emitting from the roasting joint in the oven.

'You can come and lay the table out here,' she instructed, looking at me. I jumped up from the snakes and ladders board game and placed the knives and forks down onto the kitchen table.

'We might as well eat in the kitchen. They won't be back yet,' she would state, staring through at the seldom used, dining room table. The kitchen was full of steam, and I watched her, as she opened the small fanlight window, even in the middle of winter, to let it all out. Returning to the board game I was playing with my cousin Kevin, I listened to the crashing and banging of saucepans in the kitchen, as her temper increased.

'Come and make the gravy for me,' she instructed, as she mashed the swede, adding a large knob of butter. The roast potatoes, (previously added to the meat dish) were browning, and spitting lard, alongside the joint. Cabbage was chopped, and peas were dropped, rolling across the kitchen floor. Suddenly, the kitchen went quiet, as the meal was dished up, and placed onto several plates. We were instructed to sit down and eat. Eating hungrily, I watched her fill two saucepans with water, place two large, plated dinners onto each one, add a second plate upended, to cover the meal, and with an impatient sigh, she sat down to eat with Kevin and me.

'I'm not waiting for those two forever. We will have ours,' she said, as we tucked into our meal. It was well past closing time at the pub.

We had all finished our meal when the back door was opened gingerly and two jolly travellers entered, red-faced and happy, more than ready to sit down and eat their Sunday lunch.

'What time do you call this?' she would ask, as the two men swayed on the spot, grinning like Cheshire cats.

'Lovely, Auntie Nellie,' Dad would say, tucking into his meal, as they both soon cleared their plates in record time. Then they both stood up, swaying a bit. Nunk rolled up his shirt sleeves and commenced washing up. My Dad found the tea towel, and picked up the washed plates, drying them. I put it all away, listening all the time to their jovial conversation.

My aunt sat in her armchair, with a resigned expression on her face. The two men had made a very good job of washing up and tidying the kitchen. The fanlight window was closed, and they both took up their positions in the living room. Nunk sat in his favourite armchair, left of the fireplace, my aunt in the other armchair knitting, and my dad, sat on an upright dining room chair, facing the coke fire. We two children, sat underneath the dining room table, continuing with our snakes and ladders. Within minutes, both men were sound asleep. Nunk's head was laid back, mouth open, his

Brylcremed head lolling to and fro, all over the antimacassar. Dad sat with his arms slightly folded, his chin on his chest. They were both snoring very loudly, beer aroma pervading the room.

'He's sending them over the hill,' she remarked, looking at her husband with annoyance and nodding at his loud snores and shaking her head. 'Look at them both, they are disgusting. It's enough to wake the dead. He's going to fall off that chair in a minute. I don't know why they don't go and lay down on top of the beds out of our sight,' she would add. 'Roll on the summer when we can go on a few outings,' she huffed. The radio was turned up, such was the noise emanating from the pair.

We children then put on our coats and shoes and made our way off to Sunday School. This was a walk up to the local church on Gillingham Green. Over an hour later when we returned, they were both still fast asleep.

'I'm making a cup of tea,' my aunt said loudly, as we came into the kitchen, shivering with the cold. Our voices, the boiling kettle and clatter of cups and saucers were meant to wake them both up, but to no avail. We removed our shoes and coats and tried to get nearer to the one small fire, with its little doors closed, but their legs were stretched out in front of the only source of heat in the prefab.

'Can I comb their hair?' I questioned, sensing her mood, as she loudly sighed, shaking out her knitting from her lap.

'Yes, wake them both up, I've had enough of their racket,' she replied.

I rushed excitedly into the bathroom, to look for Nunk's comb. Returning, I placed myself behind his armchair and commenced combing his very greasy hair. I combed and combed until I had combed it all up, into a tall, cone-shaped point, the grease helping to keep it upright. When I had finished, he resembled a garden gnome. My aunt returned with the tea tray, cups and saucers placing them down on the dining room table. Kevin was told to bring in the sponge cake, which was on its doily on a plate in the kitchen before the cat got his paws into it. She laughed out loud, as she glanced across at her snoring husband's pointed hair.

'Do your father's too,' she encouraged. Using the same comb, I combed dad's hair, giving him a centre parting, and made two pointed horns. He did look funny. She couldn't stop laughing. It was enough to wake them both up, and as they gazed around in bewilderment, we three laughed at them. I made my way to the bathroom, to wash the grease from my hands, and one after the other, they followed me. It was only then, that they saw what had caused the laughter, as they both gazed at themselves in the bathroom mirror.

'You look like a garden gnome, and you look like a bull,' I shouted, and we all had to agree, laughing. As we gathered around the fire, we children drank milky, weak tea, and ate sponge cake; the men were then fully awake. I realised it was just another Sunday in the prefab and would be exactly the same, probably for many years to come, except most Sunday afternoons, in both Summer and Winter, we were expected to attend Sunday School. This meant that all was quiet for the adults for a couple of hours until we returned. When dad had his Sunday meal at his sister Rose's, Nunk and Nellie would then often have a lay down on the bed when we both went off to Sunday School. That puzzled me at the time. Adults always seemed so tired in my mind.

Mr Foreman

Ann Smith

Mr Foreman was a nice man. He had been a farmer for best part of his life. He said it was in his blood. The farm he owned was no ordinary farm. It bred pigs, not your normal pigs, for these ones had won many rosettes. They were huge beasts that commanded a lot of respect.

It was Mr Foreman's misfortune that he was extremely visually impaired. His glasses were so thick that they should have carried their own health warning.

Now he was a very conscientious farmer. He never left the barns that held the pregnant sows unattended. The pens in the winter always had fresh straw in them and the piglets, once they were born, were kept warm with infra-red lamps. In very hot summers they were treated to fans to help them keep cool and there was always fresh running water for them to drink and a mud puddle for them to wallow in. They had grass fields to run in and lived, on the whole, very happily. Occasionally one of them would get grumpy, but when they did, they could run amok.

The farm office was a shed in the middle field next door to the pens. A large white boar had woken that morning, very ratty. It was one of the hottest days of the year and one of the hottest years on record. He had kicked his pen gate open and when he could not get past the metal gate to the field, had decided to force his way into the office.

Mr Foreman had bravely given chase and tried to encourage the rampaging boar to leave the shed. But he charged; knocking over Mr Foreman and as he fell, his glasses flew off. Without them poor Mr Foreman was almost blind. He scrambled around on the floor for a while but it was no use. They were nowhere to be found. He stood up and as he did, the large white, annoyed at being disturbed again, bit off his thumb and swallowed it.

The satisfied porker made himself at home in the shed while Mr Foreman was taken to hospital to have the hole sewn up as the digit could not be recovered.

His broken spectacles lay in the long grass just outside the office door while the sun beat down on the already brittle scrub and, magnified by the inch-thick glass, started a fire that burnt down the wooden structure, with all its equipment and records going back years, as well as its angry squatter.

I suppose you could say that grumpy porker had had his bacon.

Time Changes Things

Pauline Odle

It was back in the late 1960s when I was first introduced to camping. Since then, I have had various camping experiences. It started when I was a Girl Guide and there was no such thing as the health and safety requirements we know today. Our tents were made of thick green material, I think they were old army tents, the type you see in drama productions like 'Dad's Army'. We practised putting them up the week before to check they were okay to use. On the day, we had to meet at our usual meeting hall with our kit bags, ground sheet and sleeping bags. An open-sided truck turned up. We placed the tents and our personal belongings onto the truck. It had a side flap so things did not fall out. After that we were told to get on and sit wherever we could. We went 34 miles singing, and holding on tight when the truck went around the bends, in case we fell off.

On arriving we had duties to do, some put up tents or collect wood for the fire to cook, whilst others dug a hole at the end of the field. The truck helped carry bottles of water from the farm before it left us for the week. There were none of the modern facilities we know today. I had never seen cooking by fire before, and I especially enjoyed the way they cooked bananas. Leaving them in their skins but peeling the skin back, cutting the bananas sideways to put chocolate inside then fold silver foil around and put them on the fire to eat after we'd had our main course of food, it made a great pudding. Later in the evening, we made another fire. Whilst it was crackling and snapping we sat around for the closure of the evening, singing songs and drinking hot chocolate. Usually finishing with the song "Kum ba ya," whilst watching the glow of the fire and feeling the warmth it gave us, we also enjoyed looking at the stars in the night sky.

I will always remember one camp at Blacklands farm in East Grinstead. On one of our hikes, we were told to stand at the side of the road and salute. To our amazement, the car that passed us by was occupied by Olave Baden Powell, our Chief Guide and she was waving a handkerchief at us.

I have been on several really enjoyable camping trips to the Yorkshire Dales as a family when my children were young. They enjoyed the freedom this brought them and watched nature as the clouds drifted by. Although I remember two camps for the wrong reasons, this is because they made me aware of how you should not take the weather for granted. Along with the sunshine, there can be terrible destructive winds and rain. The first occasion was in 1993 when my eldest, only, child at that time was nearly four. It had been a good day but there were warnings on the radio that a storm was coming. We thought nothing of it and went to sleep as usual, until myself and then husband, awoke hearing screaming and howling winds. We looked out of the tent and could not believe the destruction we saw, or how hard it was raining. We checked on our son to find he was still sleeping peacefully. We did not sleep any more that night as we were on constant alert to what was happening. We decided that it was safer to stay where we were as the tent seemed to be holding its own against the storm. Many other tents were destroyed, and the people went to the toilet block for protection. Our tent was the only one remaining standing in the morning, but we still had to pack up and go home. Whilst the tent was okay, the water level where we were camping flooded our tent and there was no way we could dry things out enough for us to enjoy the rest of our holiday. We heard on the radio that a hotel in Scarborough had fallen into the sea by a landslide caused by the weather.

Another time soon after my youngest was born we tried the Lake District, that was a bad mistake and we never tried camping there again. The same stormy weather caused similar problems except this time there was a sewage leak somewhere. Again, we went home but this time all camping gear was unsavable and went in the bin. It was not a pleasant drive home for our noses.

My boys grew older and they joined the Scouts. As my youngest son in those days had very high special needs with a language disorder, they would only accept him provided I attended with him. Somehow, from that I found myself as a Beaver leader. At first Beavers were not allowed to go camping. However, it was our group's 100th birthday and they wanted Beavers to be part of the celebration at Gilwell Park. The group leader got special permission from the Scout Association for our Beavers, 6 to 8-year-old members of the group to be included. They were not allowed to sleep outdoors and there was a list of regulations we had to observe. To make it feel more real for them we found some tents that could be put up indoors as they did not require any ground stakes. Two adults had to always remain awake, so we took it in shifts. Thankfully the hall had a massive window from floor to ceiling in one direction so the Beavers could look at the outside world of fields whilst in their tents. It was great for me too as I will always remember the shift I had when dawn broke and the memory of watching the sun rising on the horizon will remain with me forever. I also learnt how to remember the points of a compass with the rhyme 'Naughty Elephants Squirt Water'.

I think our experience made the Scout Association rethink Beavers' camping, as soon afterwards there was a Beavers' 'night away' badge. This meant leaders had to do training for it. I was one of the first to do this to obtain my 'wood badge' that all leaders hope to gain. However, when I did this training, it had not been adjusted for Beaver leader level so I had to do the whole scout programme. I had to put up a tent in the dark. Usually, you could get tilly lamps to shine a light for you. Unfortunately, these for some reason were not available. I somehow managed to put the tent up by torch light. I did get some sleep but felt my bed was rather bumpy and it was not until the morning I realised that I had put the tent up under an oak tree and the ground was full of acorns.

Another type of camp I took my sons to was when we were learning about amateur radio. We joined a local amateur radio club that had its field days behind a local public house. We pitched our tent in the grounds of the pub and stayed overnight. There were lots of activities for us to explore and take part in at various levels. From making sundials, morse code keys, and aerials, and transmitting on various wavelengths. There was also a bar-b-que and a game of football. My sons thought it hilarious for them to wake me up at 5am to transmit and speak to a person in Australia from an aerial we helped make the day before.

What next, I wonder? Maybe I'll investigate the world of glamping as I am getting older. I like the look of these pods that are currently springing up.

Unbreakable

Judith Northwood Boorman

'Are you really sure about this?' I ask, biting my lip. 'Never been surer about anything in my whole effing life,' Tess replies, with steely resolve etched on her face, framed by an enviable abundance of curly auburn locks. Even gaunt and haggard, she is, without a doubt, one of the most beautiful women I know. She has always been petite and elfin-like, but now she has an ethereal quality; a platinum glow.

We have just completed the trip of our lifetime and are now standing outside a functional-looking building on a business estate. Rather a contrast to the previous exquisite seven days. This trip was all about the journey and not the destination. The magic commenced as soon as we boarded the gleaming Pullman at London's Victoria station. We stepped into a world of glamour, class, and affluence. Certainly not the world I frequented these days and definitely not Tess's world. Her face lit up; a radiant beacon of joy.

'OM effing G,' she exclaimed, as we sunk down on the eye-zinging, zebra-patterned upholstery. Within minutes, the smartly liveried waiter presented us with our welcome fizzing champagne.

'This definitely isn't South-Eastern Railways.' She added.

'No, in fact it doesn't belong to any railway company at all. A company called Belmond owns it. I'd never heard of them until I booked the tickets.' I replied, ever the travel agent.

'Bloody, bloody brilliant.' She grabbed both my hands in her bony grasp. 'You really are the bestest mate!'

'It's the least I could do.' I replied, fighting back the sharp prick of tears starting to form behind my aching eyelids.

Her eyes, glistening diamonds, mirrored mine.

A short stay in Venice continued this memorable journey. We had arranged our trip to coincide with the famous Venice festival. We bought two outrageous masks, rather spooky skeletons, adorned with plumes of brightly coloured feathers. We loved our new look. Seemed ironically appropriate.

Everyone we met was so joyful and friendly. We danced until Tess clung to me for support; a limp puppet with snipped strings. She loved the gondola ride, along narrow, slightly odorous, canals. Passing the flaking buildings, it revelled in its own faded grandeur. Every now and then, we'd have to duck under the low bridges. We couldn't resist the temptation of singing, 'Just one Cornetto,' and recalling the Venetian setting of our favourite film: 'Don't Look Now!'

Then the early start at Venezia Santa Lucia Station. Tess really is not an early riser. But she rose to that challenge, wearily pulling herself from the ultra-comfortable bed of the Belmond Hotel Cipriani.

We enjoyed another scenic railway journey from Venice to Zurich, with just a short wait at Milan. We started to feel like seasoned railway travellers and joked about bumping into Michael Portillo, clad in one of his eye-popping florid outfits. Sadly, we didn't. He would have made a very entertaining travelling companion.

Six hours later, the train was grinding to a juddering halt at the bustling but clinical Zurich Hauptbahnhof. Just in time for lunch.

I really hoped Tess would like the Dolder Grand Hotel as much as I had when I stayed there thirty years before. We could have taken a taxi from the station straight to the hotel but Tess was keen to walk to the 'base station' to take the quaint and more scenic, funicular. I had told her about it when I had previously related the hilarious episode at the Dolder's sister hotel, the Waldhaus.

After re-telling the story about the managers' trip, where we had worn blue smurf-like hats on our heads in the swimming pool, provoking a comment from a rather prim Swiss lady, 'Zay are for zee fuss, not zee 'ed.', we collapsed into childish giggles, attracting bemused stares from the other passengers.

That previous trip seemed a very long time ago. I had been single and career driven. Tess already had three children under the age of five and shared my trips by proxy. She loved that story, so it seemed only fitting that we should visit this iconic hotel on this ultimate adventure. Now her three girls are grown up with their own families. The eldest is my Goddaughter, Lauren.

Champagne cocktails on the Dolder Grand's panoramic patio, with its glorious vista of Zurich and the lake, was another great success. We clinked glasses.

'To life!' Tess added.

Our last morning, we dance around our spacious room to, "Adventure of a Lifetime" playing on YouTube on my phone.

'I so love that song,' she sighs, wistfully, 'It's just perfect for this trip.'

I agree, trying to dislodge the marble-sized lump forming in my throat; unwanted tears stabbing for freedom in my tear ducts.

The trip by taxi to Forch is too short, less than twenty minutes, even taking the longer route. It takes us closer to the lake, catching glimpses of the shimmering, buttery sunshine reflecting off the water's dazzling surface.

Both Tess and I are silent.

We arrive.

With trepidation, we now enter the building.

I look at Tess, but she avoids my gaze. I wonder if she, like me, has had the past seven days replaying in her brain, like an alternative screenplay to 'Don't Look Now'.

It seems quite apt. I really don't want to look now. I'd rather not be here at all, but I promised. I grit my teeth with the same steely resolve as my dearest friend. She grips my arm for support, her awkward gait and fragile frame now getting the better of her.

We enter the building. Formalities over, we are now sitting in comfortable chairs, side by side.

Our final cocktail.

We clink glasses.

'To us,' we whisper in unison, hands clenched together as if sealed by Superglue.

This concoction will halt the ticking time bombs. Tess's condition visible, unlike mine, which is secreted deep within my brain.

We will remain united for eternity.

Our bond is unbreakable.

The Day I Met Lord and Lady Carnarvon

Brenda M Moss

Due to the Covid pandemic, our planned coach trip arranged with our local History Group, to Highclere Castle in 2020, had to be cancelled. We then heard that it was going ahead for 2021 as the necessary precautions had been put in place by the management at the castle, to ensure that we all had a safe environment, in which to enjoy our trip.

Wearing masks, we left Gillingham at 8.00.am and our first stop was for a 'comfort break' at Cobham services, then sometime later, arriving in Newbury for an hour and a half lunch break. Highclere was only a 15-minute drive away and when we arrived, our driver asked us all to be back at the coach by 4.45pm for our departure.

There were four other coaches parked in the car park, some distance from the castle and hundreds of private cars. Long queues were wending their way up to the castle's welcoming wooden doors. We made our way slowly across the acres of grassland to the castle. It was whilst we were walking, that I thought that I could see someone on stilts, entertaining the queue of visitors. As we arrived, we could see that indeed there was someone dressed in a 1920's period police uniform, walking on stilts. He was entertaining the queue of visitors and making them smile with his mannerisms and funny banter. I was fascinated by his stilts and was trying to work out how he was standing on them as he moved to and fro. I then asked him whether I could feel the area where his own shoe appeared to be situated in the wide trouser bottoms.

'Can I have a feel'? I asked tentatively. He obliged and I was amazed to discover that he had a chunky pair of soft, leather-topped boots, affixed to the stilts, on which he stood. He seemed anxious to move on, perhaps he thought I was about to tickle him, and he made a joke about not being asked before by a lovely young lady if she could have a feel, which made the queue all laugh. Me too, as it has been a very long time since anyone has paid me that type of compliment. Lovely young lady indeed!

Eventually, it was our turn to enter the Castle. We were welcomed by a mature, female guide who informed us that the Queen often visited Highclere, as she had a keen interest in the horses and stables. I asked if she stayed in the castle and was told that when she visited, she usually stayed at one of the houses on the estate (probably cosier). We moved along various corridors at a snail's pace and stood outside roped-off rooms, some of which I recognised from the TV series and in those rooms they had large, mounted photographs, on easels, of the actors and actresses, taken during their scenes, either seated or standing. Most rooms had floral arrangements and my sister-in-law was very drawn to several plants, and flowers, arranged in beautiful large vases. She was particularly taken by a fiery red, floral arrangement, in a blue and white, curved, boat-shaped container. My friend Stella and I were both scrutinising the artwork, in particular, the brush strokes and my brother Ray was pointing out of a large, opened window which overlooked the vast gardens.

'Look at that,' he said gazing out.

'Yes, it is a lovely view, isn't it?' I replied as I glanced out.

'No, not the view, look at the window frames' Ray insisted.

All the windows had been left wide open to allow for air circulation throughout the castle. He was struck by how the paintwork needed attention and how the wood needed renewing. It made me smile. I suggested that he volunteered to do a window a week!

We made our way down a steep flight of stairs, (passing the dumb waiter to our left) via the kitchen (not the one to be seen in the TV series of Downton Abbey, but a modern equivalent used by caterers for weddings.) At the bottom of the stairs, the museum was situated. This had been very well displayed, with artefacts brought back from Egypt by a previous Lord Carnarvon, but also replica models of jewellery which were very well made. There were two male mannequins, one seated, the other looking over his shoulder, posing at a desk scrutinising paperwork relating to Egypt, representing Lord Carnarvon and Howard Carter who discovered the tomb of Tutankhamun. I felt that the exhibition was probably visited by local schools, as there were several items that children would find interesting and viewing holes lower down (at child level) were noted. In another corridor, glass-fronted cabinets housed the silver plate and cutlery.

'Bit different to having a tray on our laps in front of the TV,' commented my sister-in-law.

We finally left the castle and made our way outside to the tearoom. Whilst we were seated outside, enjoying a refreshing cup of tea, and cake, the jovial policeman staggered past yet again, still chatting to everyone, but this time pushing a wooden duck on wheels.

'I'm not quackers, he is,' he shouted, as he strode past. With a nod in our direction, I managed to take a couple of photographs. Very tired, my brother and sister-in-law had decided to make their way back to the coach, whilst my friend Stella and I went to the public conveniences eventually also heading back. We were both now moving very slowly and feeling very tired, when a well-spoken lady asked us if we had seen a man dressed as a policeman and we explained to her where we had last seen him. We noticed that his strange wooden bicycle was propped up in the hedge to our left, as we passed. She thanked us and walked back towards the tearoom. As we walked around the hedges, in front of us, the policeman loomed yet again, lumbering towards us. We said that a lady had been looking for him and he asked us to describe her.

'She has grey hair wearing a blue coat, about our height' we both chorused.

'Did the coat have writing on its back?' he continued. We weren't sure as we had not glanced back at her departure, as she was in a hurry.

'That's my wife' he responded, then as an afterthought, 'Lady Carnarvon'.

'If she is your wife, then you must be Lord Carnarvon,' I responded and added. 'It's not every day that we meet a Lord,' I called after him, as he too hurried away.

'Me? I'm not a Lord, I'm a policeman,' he mischievously shouted back, as he lumbered along, taking competent large strides, and staggering around the pathway between the bushes, in his urgent search for Lady Carnarvon.

My Secret Dream
A man considers his wife lost to him; through dementia

Angela Johnson

There was a woman once
who saw her dreams at dusk
with the light fading;
a luminous phosphorescence.
And in darkness; nothing.
I, the man sleeping by her side, listen,
worshipping her very breath.
I dream of her smiling, when she was with me,
not in the anarchy of her present dreams,
These mockeries of what she was
No sane morning soul laugh
to brush away like irritations on smooth skin.
Nor daytime fantasies which amuse.
Chimeras between light and dark, sleeping and waking,
Bone fingered beckonings
She floats over the earth like leaves falling and floating dust.
"I will see her smile again, she will come back."
I whisper to the silence.

Leaves

Susan Pope

Safia draws her coat closer against the sharp wind. October. The fall has begun once more in chilly England. Not like back home where the seasons ran together like sticky treacle, only the rainy one marking a difference.

Leaves fall from the oaks and plane trees in the park. She marvels at the myriad colours. Green through to brown with many shades of yellow, orange and russet-red in between, swept by the wind into circles deep and mysterious.

With a start of delight, children run under the trees whooping, shouting, and laughing. They dance in joyous circles kicking and crunching the leaves into a kaleidoscope of different patterns, the colours moving in the dance; blue jackets for school, confusing with the autumnal shades on the ground and still falling from above.

Safia shares the scene but not the dance. She isn't on the way to school, not anymore. She left that behind in July. Barely sixteen – education abandoned – no prize-gifted certificates for Safia. She is a failure, a disappointment to her family. Not like her brother; eighteen, with six A levels and more certificates than Safia can count. Kyle's gone to Kent Uni at Canterbury, a freshman living in halls. He could have stayed living at home in Canterbury. It's where Safia lives with Mum and Dad and Julia. Though home to Safia will always be with Grandma Co-Co. She loves Co-Co. She misses Co-Co.

They came here for a better life. Seems they all found it; all except Safia. She doesn't fit in anywhere.

Footnote:
University of Kent Summer School, Creative Writing presentation piece. July 2015.

Adore and Appreciate

Nilufar Imam

Banish despondency and the pessimistic situation,
Be great and be grateful,
Hope is the strength and core of all.

Express and enrich yourself as well as others,
Look within to grasp the opportunities,
Share and start joyful living.

Footnote:
First published in Searching for the Rainbow, Nilufar Imam 2022